M000041249

PROLOGUE

olt stared up at the solitary puffy white cloud in the fiercely blue sky—perfect conditions for lying in the field making big plans for the future. It seemed impossible to have such a day when Colt felt darkness calling him, but he knew his mother would have loved it. She'd have hummed under her breath as she went about her chores on the ranch, maybe even take his and his sister's hands and dance with them around the table, laughing and giddy with happiness.

Anything was more suited to this day than this. A numbness held him comfortingly close as he stared across from where he sat, the preacher extolling his mother's virtues as she lay cold and stiff in her coffin. Beside Colt, his kid sister, Indie, sniffled, her slight shoulders shaking as if her sorrow shuddered and shook to be free. Suddenly feeling older than his almost eighteen years, he wrapped an arm around her. The preacher continued to drone on, his words washing over Colt as though his brain reached out to grasp them but they slipped through like wisps of smoke, intangible to his grieving mind.

Woodenly, Colt rose to his feet when directed, helping

Indie stand. A sudden growth spurt meant that her fifteen-year-old head didn't quite make his shoulders. She clung to his hand as if fearful that, if she let go, he would disappear too. They walked together to the edge of the freshly dug grave their mother had just been lowered into, each pausing before tossing in a white carnation—their mother's favorite flower. Colt swallowed hard, battling against the rising tsunami of grief. He would not let the town gossips have anything to discuss and dissect over their glasses of sweet tea. Gently and with head held high, Colt guided his sister toward his pickup, a temporary reprieve before the funeral attendees would gather at the ranch for the wake.

"I don't think I can do this, Colt," Indie said in a tiny voice, long gone husky from crying. "When Dad died, it was hard, but we still had Mom. What are we going to do now?" Her bottom lip quivered as fresh tears streamed down her face.

Resolve hardened in the pit of Colt's stomach. He was all she had left now, and there was nothing he wasn't going to do for her. "Indie, we've got each other. Dad left us enough money to get by, and I've been doing real good on the local circuit with my roping. In a few years, I might just be good enough to go pro. At least, that's what Mom said." He felt a fresh stab of pain at the thought of his mom. "And she should know. She spent a heck of a lot of time following Dad around on the circuit."

"But I still need to finish school. You can't go and leave me," Indie wailed, fear making her eyes huge in her pale face.

"Indie, I'm not going anywhere. At least not for a few years. And by then, you'll probably be heading off to college or something."

Colt turned down the familiar dirt drive, the house beckoning him as he rattled past horses and cattle grazing in the fields. Pulling up, he turned the ignition off and sat,

THE WOUNDED COWBOY BILLIONAIRE

BILLIONAIRE HEARTS SERIES BOOK ONE

EDITH MACKENZIE

This is a work of fiction. Names, **characters**, businesses, places, events, locales, and incidents are either the products of the author's imagination or used in a fictitious manner. Any resemblance to actual persons, living or dead, or actual events is purely coincidental

The Wounded Cowboy Billionaire(Billionaire Hearts Ranch Book #1):

Images © DepositPhotos – pikselstock & Kotenko. Cover Design © <u>Designed with Grace</u>

❀ Created with Vellum

The pain of grief never leaves you when you lose someone you love. You just get used to carrying the burden. I miss you Dad xx

breathing deeply. When he walked through the door, there would be no smell of freshly baked cookies or music playing from the radio. No warm smile or hand to tousle his hair and remark once again—in surprise, like it was the first time— just when had he gotten so big, that only yesterday he'd come up to her hip. No, this time the house would be cold and empty.

A battered pickup ground to a halt beside Colt's car. Two teenage boys stepped out and stood kicking the dirt, hands thrust into the pockets of their jeans. Somehow, he'd known that his two best friends would be the first to arrive. Taking in one last steadying breath, he opened his door.

"Come on, Indie, we're home." She gave a quick nod and slid out, standing forlorn beside the truck. Bennett, one of Colt's best friends, quickly went around to her, and she smiled sadly at him, her braces catching the light.

"You might want to watch him," Logan said, his joking tone strained as if uncertain how to act. "I'm not sure I'd want him around my kid sister."

"I wouldn't want you around my kid sister either. Bennett, I can trust. He's just being a good friend." Colt watched an old Volkswagen Beetle bounce down the drive. "Anyway, he hasn't got a chance once her friends arrive. Speaking of which, how did your date with Misty go?"

Logan straightened with all the cocky dignity a seven-teen-year-old boy possessed. "A gentleman never kisses and tells." He winked at Colt.

"Last time I checked, you're no gentleman. At least, that's what Suzie Masterson says."

"Well, Suzie Masterson ain't no lady the last time I checked either," Logan retorted, waving the dust the tires of the Volkswagen had sent flying through the air as it came to a stop and two teenage girls stepped out. "Hey, Misty."

A cute little brunette waved shyly at him. "Hi, Logan."

Her friend smiled at Colt, the compassion shining from her eyes almost bringing him undone. "We're real sorry about your mom. My ma wants you to know that if there's anything you need, just let her know."

Colt nodded, not trusting himself to speak, watching as Evelyn gave him another sad little smile before heading over to his sister. Bennett, suddenly finding himself outnumbered, surrendered and re-joined his friends.

"You look like a rooster who just got thrown out of the hen house." Logan nudged his friend.

"Quit it, Logan. I was just seeing how Indie was holding up. She's got her friends now, so I came back." Bennett sent cow eyes back over to the object of his affections.

Later as Colt stood beside his sister, accepting condolences from mourners, he was grateful for that moment of normalcy. Now as murmured conversation swirled around him, a gray tinge to a room that had always been filled with laughter and light, he wanted to demand that everyone get out. He wanted to kick and shout and punch the wall. Instead, he smiled and nodded as people stopped to pay their respects. The strong perfume of the church ladies mingled with the tobacco smell wafting off old Mr Peterson's clothes, making the air too hard to breathe. Colt's face felt stiff from trying to maintain a fake smile while refraining from crying. He just wanted his mom back. He wanted her to tell him everything was going to be okay and then wrap him in her warm arms and sing softly until it became true.

"They say it was a heart attack, but we all know it was a broken heart," Bessy Warren murmured behind a sandwich to her fellow gossip, Rosie Smith. "After he passed away from cancer, we all knew it wouldn't be long before she joined him. Such a shame with the children and all."

Rage made Colt tremble. *How dare they talk about his mom like she chose to die, that she chose to leave them behind.* Setting down the delicate teacup he held in his hand for fear of breaking it, he cleared his throat.

"My sister and I would like to thank everyone for coming today. I know Mom would have been happy to know how loved she was, but now we would like to spend some time remembering her privately. Mrs Warren, Mrs Smith, I believe you both know where the door is."

The ladies in question huffed, scandalized that they were being asked to leave. "He's only going to get worse without the refining hand of a mother," Rosie Smith whispered behind her hand to her accomplice.

"If everyone could please follow them, we thank you for your understanding in this trying time." Colt ignored Indie's questioning look from across the room where she was safely ensconced on the sofa between Evelyn and Misty. He stood, counting each breath in and out until the room was empty except for their friends and themselves.

"You want us to leave, too?" asked Bennett, a fragile plate piled high with sandwiches and cookies.

"No, you guys are family. I just couldn't take it with the old busybodies who were only here to pick over Mom's dead body like vultures." Evelyn scooted over to make space for Colt beside Indie.

He wrapped his arm around his sister, and she burrowed into him like a little kitten. "Nothing's going to be all right ever again, is it?" Her quiet voice made his heart clench unbearably.

"I promise you, Indie, I'm going to make sure you have the best life. You and me, we're going to make Dad and Mom so proud. And when we're old, we're gonna sit on the porch out the front like Dad used to and tell our grandkids all about the adventures of their great-grandpa and grandma."

Indie gave a sad little sigh. "Sometimes I wonder if I'm my

mother's daughter. But right now, all I want to do is go to bed and pretend like none of this ever happened."

Colt closed his eyes against the sting of tears. Maybe she was right. Tomorrow he would wake up and it would all be a bad dream. Somehow his seventeen-year-old heart doubted it.

CHAPTER 1

*T*he sky was clean and bright with faint wisps of clouds like cotton candy dotted about. Colt swung the rope experimentally as he walked his horse around, warming up his arm, the smell of livestock and dust filling the air. The cute cowgirl coming the other way recognized him, her eyes widening gratifyingly and her gaze dropping to take in his gleaming gold world champion buckle. He sent her his best slow and lazy smile, cocking his head as he appraised her appreciatively, promising himself he would catch up with her later and get to know her better.

It was a good day to be alive. Big Wheels, his horse, was calm and steady beneath him, too much of an old rodeo hand to be bothered with nerves. A movement at the edge of the warmup area caught his attention. Standing to her full five-foot, three inches height, his sister waved, pausing to see if he'd noticed her before setting off waving again. Beside Indie and standing tall was his best friend—her fiancé—Bennett. Grinning at them, he loped Big Wheels over.

"I didn't expect to see you guys here. I hope someone is looking after my ranch."

Indie cocked her head at him. "The ranch is fine, and it's *our* ranch. Maybe we just wanted to come and spend some time with you. You know, live the playboy billionaire lifestyle." She looked up at Bennett, a silly smile on her face. "Can we just tell him already?"

Bennett's smile was just as goofy. "If you don't, I will."

"Is someone going to tell me? Why didn't you just call if you had something to say?" His sister looked like she was about to explode with whatever news she had to tell. Maybe he should torment her a little longer, string it out. Really, what kind of big brother wouldn't take advantage of this situation?

"We didn't want to tell you over the phone. This is something that I wanted to see your face when we told you. You're the only family I have, and I want to do this right." Indie seemed torn between blurting her news out or crying.

"You guys didn't run off and get married, did you? Bennett, you and I are going to have words if you didn't give my little sister the big wedding she's always dreamed of."

Bennet exchanged a knowing look with him. "You think she'd let me get away with an elopement?"

Colt chuckled. "Maybe not. So, what's this big news you're all fired up to tell me about?"

Indie's eyes shimmered with excitement. She clutched at Bennett's arm as if to anchor herself and not get carried away with her emotions. "Colt, I'm pregnant. We're going to be having a baby." Colt felt like he'd been poleaxed. His baby sister was going to be a mom. A wave of bittersweetness hit him. *Mom would have loved being a grandma.* "You're happy for us, aren't you, Colt?" Indie's eyes no longer shimmered with excitement. Now the tears that had threatened clung perilously to her lashes.

"You caught me by surprise, but I like the idea of being Uncle Colt." He slid off his horse and wrapped her up in a giant bear hug. "You're going to make the best mom," he whispered in her ear. He shook Bennett's hand. "Congratulations. I'm over the moon for you guys."

Bennett's grip was firm. "Thanks. You know I'll make sure they never want for anything."

"If I'd had my doubts, I wouldn't have let you anywhere near her when we were in high school." Colt's name crackled over the loudspeaker. "I'm next in. Are you guys staying around?"

"Yeah, this one here"—Bennett smiled lovingly down at Indie—"informs me that she already has cravings. So we'll stay for the rodeo and then head home afterwards."

Indie punched her fiancé lightly on the arm. "Hey, mister, these cravings are real. Now, enough with this chit-chat. Colt, go catch a steer, and you"—she crooked her finger at Bennett—"need to go hunt me down some pickles, corndogs and ice cream."

"That seems fair enough," Colt said, climbing back into the saddle.

"She plans on eating them all together like one big, pickle corndog sundae." Bennett shuddered at the thought.

Colt grimaced, staring in horror at his sister. "Indie, that's gross."

"And I don't care. Now, git." She shooed him away with her hands.

Colt could feel a gooey smile on his face. Well, how about that? His baby sister was having a baby—and with one of his best friends, no less.

~

"I SWEAR I thought that bull was going to put a hole in your backside." Bennett swiped at his eyes, laughing heartily at his friend's expense.

"Ain't no way that bull was faster than me. Heck, I was in that barrel before he even knew which way I'd gone," denied Logan. Loud laughter from the bar broke through the music playing from the jukebox as he re-enacted his zigzag escape from the bovine's attention.

"Let it never be said that Logan wasn't fast when it came to running away from danger." Colt took a slug from his beer, ducking playfully from his friend's jab to the ribs.

"Speaking of running away, I sure as heck wouldn't be running away from that pretty little blonde over there like you are." Logan rolled his eyes from the woman in question back to his friend.

Suddenly getting a drink at the bar after the rodeo had finished didn't seem like such a great idea. Especially with the way Indie was eyeballing him, her look only slightly scarier than the blonde's.

Colt coughed uncomfortably, looking sheepishly at the raised brows of his sister sitting beside her fiancé. "Um, well, it's not quite like that."

"Oh, what is it like then?" Indie asked, dunking some onion rings into her chocolate sundae. "Actually, maybe I should go over there and introduce myself." She made to stand.

"Don't you dare, sis!" Colt made a grab for her arm which she nimbly dodged, moving her food safely out of reach at the same time. He shuddered at the thought of what she was heartily wolfing down. "Let's just say that our friendship was of a fleeting nature and there's no need to get family involved."

"A fleeting nature? Is that what it's called these days?" Bennett grinned at his friend. "I mean, I'm no expert. I was lucky enough to find the woman who holds my heart straight out of the gates. But Logan, is that what you would call it?"

"I mean, I've never used those exact words myself." Logan stroked his chin thoughtfully, his eyes twinkling with mischief. "But I guess it's one way of describing it."

"Colt, did you lead her on?" Indie demanded, her eyes narrowing at her brother.

"No. I mean, I don't really remember putting that much effort into it full stop." Colt shrugged. He never had to. The ladies seemed to always be around and willing.

"Colt Montgomery!" Indie pushed her empty plastic dish away from her. "One day, you're going to meet a lady and fall hard, and she won't want anything to do with you because of your reputation." She gave a wicked little smile. "And I hope I'll be there to see it." She patted her belly. "Now, this baby and I have had enough to eat, and I think it's time for us to head home." Indie laid her head on Bennett's shoulder, gazing up at him adoringly.

Colt couldn't resist giving a teasing shake of his head at the loved-up couple in front of him. The fact that two of his favorite people in the whole dang world were having a baby made him want to give a holler. It wasn't something he wanted to do. Heck, after tonight, he was headed further up the road, hauling his horses, ready for another rodeo and then another the night after that. That was the life of a rodeo champion. Always a different town, a different blonde or brunette or sometimes a redhead, and always the buckle. *And these guys waiting for me when I get home.*

"You fellas heard little Mama here. Time to get her home." Bennett stood and extended his hand toward Colt. "You rode well tonight, but then again, when don't you?"

"It's sickening how good he is," Logan agreed. "Mr Perfect."

"Well, someone has to be. I don't see either of you two stepping up to take the burden of perfection off my shoulders." Colt lounged back in the chair, his long legs sprawled out in front of him.

"But they're such broad, manly shoulders that make all the gals sigh." Logan fluttered his eyelashes at Colt.

"Oh gosh, don't start. He's got a big enough ego as it is," protested Indie, laughing. "You don't have to live with him, but Bennet and I do. He'll be insufferable now."

"Come over here and give your insufferable big brother a hug." Colt opened his arms wide, his sister bending down to comply. "You won't be doing that before long."

"Then I'll be the one snapping my fingers every time I want a hug." Indie stepped back as Bennett clasped Colt's hand.

"Take good care of my sister," Colt said as he always did, safe in the knowledge that no harm would come to her while his best friend was around.

"Always do."

Colt watched them leave the bar, shaking his head once again at the thought of his best friend and little sister becoming parents. "I guess we should have a drink for the parents to be," he suggested to Logan.

"It's like you were reading my mind." Logan put his fingers to his temple and pulled an exaggerated thinking face. "And now what am I thinking?"

"That it's my round, just like usual." Laughing, Colt stood, making his way over to the bar. Feeling jubilant, he gave the cute brunette working behind it a wink. After all, he did have a few things to celebrate that night, and judging by the saucy smile she sent his way, the night wasn't over yet.

CHAPTER 2

*B*ands of copper and gold rippled across the deep red of the chestnut horse's hide as it impatiently pawed at the ground beside the trailer. Big Wheels had always been in tune with Colt and now seemed to be picking up on his frustration at not being on the road already.

"So, Colt." The brunette twisted her hair around her finger as she smiled coyly up at him, the effect slightly ruined by the caked-on makeup that had looked sultry last night but now looked fake and cheap. "If I give you my number, will I hear from you?"

"Being on the road can get lonely." Colt gently removed the tortured tendril from her grasp. "It sure would be nice to have someone to talk to when the nights get cold and lonesome."

Her eyes grew huge as if overwhelmed at the prospect that her reflected glory of being seen with the famous cowboy could somehow be extended. She quickly wrote her number down on a piece of paper and handed it to him as Logan sauntered into view, definitely looking the worse for wear.

"You ever want someone to warm that cold bed, give me a call." She gave him a slow, lazy look running the length of his saddle-hardened body. "Day or night." With a final suggestive glance over her shoulder, she sashayed away.

"Sure does get lonesome being a big, bad cowboy," Logan teased, fluttering his eyelashes at his friend.

"You're just sore that you slept in a cold bed by yourself."

Colt untied his horse from the side of the trailer. Big Wheels nudged him hard in the small of his back as if to say, 'About time, I thought she was never going to leave.'

"You and me both," he muttered, rubbing the chestnut's head.

"I just don't understand, when the obviously better-looking cowboy is standing right here"—Logan gestured at himself—"why you get all the attention. Maybe it's true what they say. Fame can make even the ugliest of people pretty."

"Money helps, too."

"See, I reckon it would, but I'm not sure any of these buckle bunnies have a clue about what you're actually worth. Heck, I'm not sure I even do."

The sharp ring of Colt's phone cut off his retort to his friend, a feeling of dread washing over him when it displayed a private number. *Surely she can't be calling to find out if I'm lonely already.* "Hello?"

"Is that Colt Montgomery?" a gruff, official voice said—one Colt didn't recognize. It definitely wasn't the brunette.

"Yeah, who's asking?"

"This is Officer Watson of the Mansfield Police Department. Is Indie Montgomery your sister?"

In the background, Colt could still hear Logan yammering away to Big Wheels, a horse somewhere whinnying. Stomach-churning foreboding washed everything to a dull gray around him. "Yes, I am. Is she all right?"

"She's in a stable condition. The hospital will be able to

give you a full report when you arrive. If you have a pen and paper, I can give the details of where she is."

Colt's heart froze, his lungs suddenly no longer drawing air. "Why aren't you calling Bennett? He should be with her. They left together. He's her fiancé."

"There was a car accident. When you reach the hospital, I'll make sure to be available to give you all the information."

"Is Bennett in the hospital with Indie?"

"No, sir. I'm sorry, he isn't." A catch, the briefest hesitation, was the only warning of impending doom.

"What do you mean he isn't there? They're never apart." Fear ripped the words from his throat. Big Wheels threw his head up in alarm, knocking Logan's hat from his head. "You tell me right now. Where's Bennett?"

"I'm sorry. He didn't make it."

THE FUEL GAUGE needle hovered south of empty on the beaten-up old pickup. *Why the heck couldn't Logan even manage to do simple things like keeping a full tank of gas in his truck?* Colt wanted to slam his hands on the steering wheel in frustration. He didn't have time to pull over. He didn't have time to stop. He just didn't have time.

The lead weight in his chest pulled him down, making it impossible to breathe. The truck glided to a halt on the side of the road, Colt not sure if it had simply drifted off or if he'd somehow made the decision. He went to wind down the window, desperately needing fresh air, only to find the crank handle broken off. *Darn it, Logan!* He glanced around, spying a sign in the distance. *Still fifty miles to the hospital. You better get it together before you see her. She's going to need you to be strong.*

But how? Bennett had been his best friend. This wasn't

how it was meant to be. He and Logan were meant to be planning Bennett's buck's party, making arrangements to paint him green and leave him in the woods the night before the wedding. Not planning his…

Colt pulled his mind back. He couldn't handle that, not right now. Grinding the old truck into gear, he pulled back onto the road, gratefulness overriding his frustration that Logan had offered to drive his truck and trailer home. *At least I know Big Wheels is in good hands.* Grimly, he gripped the wheel, anxiously hoping he had enough gas to make it to the next truck stop. Somehow, if he remained focused on the immediate issues, he could keep his grief at bay.

THE SMELL of strong bleach and antiseptic made Colt's stomach heave, nauseous as he was buffeted by the memories. His dad, once tanned by the sun and strong, lying sunken, all color leeched from his cheeks. The ambulance pulling away as the doors closed on the paramedics working on his mom. Clenching his teeth, he forced the bile down and strode to the counter, setting his hat down on it. *That blandly polite expression must be something they learn on the first day*, Colt thought sourly, his heartbeat erratic.

"I'm here to see Indie Montgomery. I'm her brother." He cast his gaze around the room, desperately striving to maintain some semblance of calm.

The receptionist typed away on her keyboard. "Ah, yes, she's in room 213. If you go down the corridor, you'll see some elevator doors about midway. They'll take you to the floor you want."

Colt nodded, gathering his hat, and headed in the direction she'd indicated. Surprisingly, her instructions were accurate, and he found himself standing in another corridor, staring at the black etched *213* on the door. Below it, written on a tag, was *Montgomery*. Colt dug his clammy fingers into the denim on his legs. He knew he needed to go in there and console his sister, to help her—heck, make sure she was okay herself—but his legs were paralyzed.

"Excuse me, are you lost?" an older looking nurse asked, her tone calm and soothing as if seeing a grown man standing in the corridor with a lost expression was an everyday occurrence. *It probably was.*

"No, ma'am."

She looked from him to the door and back again. "Are you the young lady's family?"

"Brother."

"I see. I'm about to go in there to do a check on her. If you like, we can both go in together."

It felt like the first day of school. When he'd been terrified to enter, Mrs Norris had held his hand and led him across the threshold of the classroom. Heck, that had been the day he'd met Logan and Bennett for the first time. A fresh wave of grief stabbed at him. "Ma'am, how is she?" Colt's voice was husky with emotion.

"She knocked her head pretty bad and has some stitches."

"Does she know? About…" Colt couldn't bring himself to actually say it.

"Yes. I have to warn you, we had to sedate her to keep her calm for her baby's sake. The last time I checked on her, she was still heavily under its effects, but I know she'll be reassured to have you in there with her."

Guilt gnawed at him. He was standing out here when his kid sister needed him in there with her. "I'm ready to go in." He looked down at the gray linoleum floor, desperately pushing all his emotions down. He swallowed over the lump in his throat and looked back up at her. "When you are."

The nurse smiled gently at him. Another time, he would

have noticed how kind her tired eyes were and how the deep creases around them spoke of laughter and smiles. But not today, not now. She pushed open the door and stepped through. "Indie, I have someone you'll be pleased to see."

The impersonal room was dimly lit, a soft bedside lamp the only source of lighting except for backlit buttons on the wall above Indie's bed. The bedsheets rustled as his sister stirred, rousing her mind from wherever it had wandered.

"Bennett?" That single word cut through Colt like a knife.

"Hi, Indie. It's me, Colt."

A soft sob escaped her. "I knew it couldn't be Bennett. Did they tell you? He's dead." Her voice started to rise, pushing through the fog of the sedation. "There was so much blood, Colt." Great racking shudders tore through her body. "What am I going to do, Colt? What am I going to do without him?"

Colt took his sister into his arms and held her. "I'm so sorry, Indie." But the words were inadequate, and the loss of Bennett immeasurable.

The nurse quietly walked to the other side of the bed, having checked the chart at the foot of it. "Indie, you need to listen to me. You have to calm down."

Indie pulled back from Colt, her eyes wild. "Colt, what happens if my baby isn't okay? What happens if it's hurt, too?"

Colt looked at the nurse for reassurance, panic rising up and grabbing a fistful of his insides that he wouldn't know the right thing to say. "I'm sure the doctors have checked to make sure everything is fine. Haven't they?"

"We're monitoring the situation," the nurse calmly replied, fixing a blood pressure cuff to his sister's arm.

"What does that mean? Monitoring?" Colt knew his voice was too sharp when the nurse had shown nothing but kindness, but fear drove him, lashing at him.

"We've carried out initial checks, but the baby and its mother"—the nurse smiled kindly at Indie, tears still silently tracking down her face—"will require monitoring before we can safely say either is out of the woods. A doctor will be by shortly to answer any questions you might have." With a final note of the chart, she released the cuff, returning it to the machine, and quietly departed the room.

"Bennett," whimpered Indie brokenly. "I want Bennett."

"I know. I wish I could make everything better."

He held his sister's hand until she fell into an exhausted sleep, tossing fretfully. He gently extracted his hand and stepped out into the corridor, pulling his phone out of his pocket. He dialed a number that he honestly couldn't remember when he'd last called it.

"Hello? Is that you, Colt?" It was a woman's voice, the Texan twang softened by a slightly more cosmopolitan accent, a hint of Italian, a smidge of English.

"Yeah, it's me. Evelyn, Indie needs you and Misty." His voice broke and he swallowed, the vice tightening around his chest.

"Anything she needs, we're there for, but what happened? Colt, are you okay?" Concern threaded each word.

"I, ah, Indie's in hospital. She was in an accident. They want to keep her here for a while." Tears stung his eyes as the bland wall in front of him blurred.

"Misty and I will be there as soon as we can. Is Bennett with her now?"

"Ah—" The lump in his throat bottled the words up. "Bennett's dead."

There was nothing but silence on the other end of the phone. "Oh, Colt," Evelyn breathed, shocked sorrow permeating each word. "I—how—I don't know what to say." Her voice sounded choked. "Indie must be a mess."

"Yeah."

"Colt, how are you?"

He blinked, surprised that she would ask after him. Indie was the one who needed everyone's focus. "I'm—I can't really think about it right now."

"I understand. I'll call Misty, and we'll be there as soon as we can. And Colt?"

"Yeah?"

"I'm sorry. I know he was your best friend, too."

Colt walked back to Indie's room, slumped under the burden of the grief stacked upon him. She gave a little whimper as he sat down as if, even in sleep, she couldn't escape the pain of her loss. He silently buried his face in his hands and sobbed—for her, for Bennett and their baby, and for himself.

CHAPTER 3

*C*olt looked around with satisfaction at the expensive private room he'd had Indie upgraded to. The other nurse had seemed nice, but here his sister had her own nurse to look after her instead of an entire ward. After a brief discussion with her doctor, it had been decided to lighten her sedation. *Today, tomorrow, next week. It doesn't matter when she comes off it, she's still going to hurt. I wish—heck, there ain't no use in wishing for something that ain't gonna happen.*

A tentative knock sounded on the door and a small, dark-haired woman entered the room, concern radiating from her periwinkle blue eyes. "Colt," the woman said, her lovely heart-shaped face sad. "We came as quickly as we could. Luckily, Misty's private plane was fueled and ready to go."

Colt stood and took the slight woman in his arms before releasing her to hug the other woman who was hot on her heels. "Evelyn, Misty, I'm real glad you're here." He gestured for them to take the chairs beside the bed.

"How is she?" The dark-haired Evelyn asked, gently brushing some strands of hair from the slumbering Indie's face.

"They say she can go home sometime tomorrow, and as far as they can tell, the baby is fine. She has to come back next week for more checks for the baby, but otherwise..." Colt thrust his hands deep into his pockets. "She hasn't had her sedation topped up, but all she does is sleep."

"Trying to escape reality," Misty murmured sympathetically, stroking her sleeping friend's hand.

"Hey." Indie blinked slowly as if even the dim lights were too bright for her.

"Hey, yourself," Misty said, a little too upbeat.

Indie licked her dry lips and Evelyn quickly poured a glass of water for her from the jug on her nightstand. "Did Colt tell you?"

"Oh, Indie, we're so sorry," Evelyn said as her and Misty both reached out to their friend. Colt felt like an intruder, the bonds between the women reaching Indie in a way he hadn't been able to while still wrapped in his own grief for his best friend.

"Somehow it feels like he's still here with me. When I close my eyes, I can sense him beside me, keeping me and the baby safe." Indie's voice choked with unshed tears. "I'm not imagining it, am I?"

"No." Misty glanced briefly at Evelyn, an indecipherable look passing between them. "Since you were fifteen and still wearing braces on your teeth, Bennett never left your side. I don't imagine he would start now."

The thought of a ghostly Bennett hovering about seemed to give Indie comfort and she let out a soft sigh. "I hated those braces, but he always said he thought I looked cute with them."

"I always told him to stop calling my kid sister cute," Colt growled. "But he never did listen to me where you were concerned."

"You were such an overprotective big brother, too, always prowling around." Evelyn giggled.

Somehow the sound lightened the room, and then it crashed in on Colt again. Bennett was dead. He spun on his heels and bolted from the room.

"Colt!" Indie called after him, but there was no way he was staying in there and letting her see him cry.

He made it down the corridor to a visitor's lounge, a startled couple looking up from their outdated magazines at his wild arrival as he heaved in giant gulps. Soon, the very air seemed to change, the stale, sterile odor replaced with a light floral fragrance.

"Colt?" Evelyn laid a hand gently on his shoulder.

"I just need a minute to myself." He couldn't bear to look at her. He was Colt Montgomery, champion roper, billionaire, and no one had seen him cry in public since his mom's funeral.

"I understand, but I wanted you to know that you're not alone. We're here for Indie, but we're here for you, too." Her soft voice was almost his undoing. All Colt could do was nod, not trusting his voice. "I'm going to go back in with Indie now."

He nodded again and reached up to clasp her hand where it rested lightly on his shoulder. For a moment, they stood, not needing to talk, and then she was gone, leaving him to his sorrow.

INDIE LAID with her head rolled to one side, her complexion chalky as she stared off into the distance. Evelyn could only begin to imagine the depths of her despair. She glanced toward the door again, wondering if she should go out and check on Colt again. Tall, strong Colt. The cowboy with the magic smile and the golden touch. Seeing him bowed down in the visitor's lounge had broken her heart.

"Indie, Colt told me that you can go home tomorrow," Misty said.

With her eyes wide, she looked like she was trying to telepathically communicate with Evelyn, urging her to join the one-sided conversation. *I guess she doesn't want us sitting in silence.*

"Yeah, he told me the same thing." Evelyn cast her mind around for something else to say. "I bet it'll feel good to get out of that hospital bed and eat some real food."

"Indie, look what the cat dragged in." Colt entered the room, Logan trailing behind him, hat in hand.

"How you feelin', Indie?" Logan asked, his gaze rigidly fixed on the patient.

Indie barely raised her gaze from her hands. "A little better today."

Evelyn rose gracefully from her chair and went to hug Logan. "How are you holding up?"

"Mighty glad to not be driving, but I did get a hankering for a truck as flash as Colt's. A man could get used to driving something like that."

"If you got a real job, you could afford to buy yourself a nice truck. Are you still driving that beat-up rust bucket?" Misty said, giving him a flat, unfriendly look.

"He sure is. I drove it here myself," Colt said. "I got lots of fresh air, what with all the holes in it."

"She goes, and that's all that matters," Logan said, defending his vehicle and avoiding looking directly at Misty.

"Well, you'd know a thing or two about going, wouldn't you?" Misty narrowed her eyes at him.

"Okay, guys, this isn't really the time or place for this." Evelyn was worried that, if she didn't break it up soon, there were going to be punches thrown.

"I'm feeling a little tired." Indie's wan voice had Logan shuffling his feet awkwardly and Misty staring at her hands in her lap. *Seriously, they're like little kids sometimes.*

"Do you want us to stay with you?" Colt asked, pushing past Logan to get closer to his sister.

She smiled at him, her eyes already drooping shut. "I think I might like to be alone for a while."

Evelyn's heart squeezed painfully as she trooped out with everyone else. There had been a sad acceptance in the way Indie had said it. *Alone.* Like this was her future now.

RAW ANGUISH FILLED every second of the tortured "No!" that was ripped from Indie's throat as her knees crumpled from under her. Evelyn rushed to her fallen friend, giving Misty a traumatized look on her other side.

"Indie, if you don't want to be here, I'm sure there are plenty of other rooms that Colt would be more than happy for you to use." Evelyn wanted to slap herself for not considering that this would be her friend's reaction to returning to the suite of rooms her and Bennett had shared.

Everything about the space showed glimpses of the man who had lived there, and they hadn't even made it to the bedroom yet. Some of his hats hung on hooks along one wall beside framed photographs of Indie and him in happier times, a plush looking rug thrown over the back of the black sofa. Evelyn could picture them snuggled up together watching the television, content in their private space in Colt's mansion.

"No." Indie sniffed, her words barely legible. "I want to be in here. I need to be here, where I can still feel him. I just can't do it alone. It hurts too much." Shakily, she rose to her feet, her friends hovering anxiously about her. "Can you stay with me?"

"Of course," Misty said.

Pride at her friend's courage made tears burn Evelyn's eyes as Indie drew a shaky breath and, trembling chin raised, slowly shuffled toward the bedroom. The girls followed her over to the bed, and Misty pulled the covers back for Indie to climb in. Traces of a man's aftershave tickled Evelyn's nose, hauntingly elusive, never to return again. A room of happiness and love now cold and empty.

Indie hugged a pillow tightly to her, burying her face into it as shuddering sobs racked her body. The source of the aftershave was stronger now. Obviously the pillow Indie clutched so desperately smelled of him. Misty and Evelyn climbed in on each side of her and wrapped their grieving friend tightly in their arms, knowing there was nothing they could do to ease her torment but not willing to allow her to do it alone either. It was only after many hours later that her tears had been spent and she fell into an exhausted sleep. Still awake, Evelyn wondered who was holding Colt.

CHAPTER 4

*N*o parent should ever have to bury a child. Bennet had been a late-in-life surprise, which Evelyn suspected is why he got away with so much. Now, sitting across from the table of the elderly couple, she wondered how on earth they'd manage to go on in their twilight years. Sandwiched between her and Misty, Indie sat rigidly upright, her features drawn, deep purple smudges under her eyes. The kitchen curtains stirred lightly in the morning breeze as light reflected off the shiny Italian marble kitchen counter, but nothing could dispel the heavy atmosphere of the sunny room. *Heck, a stiff breeze, and Indie's liable to shatter.*

Bennett's mother placed her cup of coffee down on the table. The tremor racking her hand set the contents to splashing over the rim and down the side. A dark ever-expanding puddle marred the expensive polished timber of the table.

"I'm so sorry." Tears choked her voice, and she pulled a tissue from her bag to mop at the mess.

Misty sprang into action, taking the cloth from the

grieving woman's hand and tidying up. "I'll do that, Mrs Gray."

The elderly woman patted Misty's hand with her own wrinkled one, now marred with spots and gnarled with age. "Thank you, dear, I just can't quite … things have just been…" Her voice trailed off. And how was the poor woman meant to find words to express the inexpressible? The death of her child, taken so cruelly from her. How was she to make sense of it?

Evelyn glanced out the window, afraid she would not be able to hold her own tears back in the face of Mrs Gray's anguish. Mr Gray hadn't spoken a word since they'd sat down, his mouth trembling from time to time, his old eyes watering. Out in the distance, she could make out Colt tending to his horses. He'd obviously slipped out early to escape having to be there for the planning of Bennett's funeral. It was hard to be angry with him when he was obviously hurting so much, but hiding from what needed to be done … well, that wasn't going to help him either.

"Mr and Mrs Gray, Indie, I know this is hard for everyone, but have you given a thought to what you would like for Bennett's funeral?" Evelyn asked as gently as she could.

Mr Gray bowed his head low, his burden too heavy for his thin neck. "I don't rightly know where to begin."

"We would want his pastor to do the service. He's known Bennett since he was a boy," Mrs Gray added.

Misty began to take notes on her tablet. "I can get the details and arrange for him to meet with you and Indie."

"I can't do this." Indie's eyes were wild, shimmering with the tears that had still to fall down her cheeks.

Evelyn put her arms around her and pulled the distraught woman in close. "Honey, none of us do, but we need to."

Indie pushed her away. "No, I'm not doing this." She sprung to her feet and dashed from the room, sobbing.

Mr Gray rubbed a hand over his tired face. "That poor gal. You were both there. There never was anyone else for either of them." He smiled sadly at his wife. "We used to say they were just like two peas in a pod. And now..." He left it unfinished. After all, what more could he say? What they were all thinking? How was Indie going to make it without him? How was she going to live when one half of her soul had been ripped away? And then there was the baby—a blessing, but now too overshadowed by the pain of loss.

Wearily, Evelyn rose to her feet. "If you'll excuse me, I don't think she should be alone. Misty, you have everything under control here?"

Her friend gave her a tight little nod. "I'm sure I can get enough to start."

With a final sad smile to the grieving parents, Evelyn slipped out of the room, wondering if she would have time to mourn Bennett herself.

She found Indie sitting on the bed, clutching the pillow to her chest, the fabric at the top damp from her tears. "I can't do it," Indie said before Evelyn could utter a single word.

Evelyn sat down beside her. "I know."

"I mean it. I can't sit there and hear how everything is going to be planned out, how the pastor is going to say nice things about him from when he was little. I mean, he was a horrible kid."

She smiled. "Hey, I remember you used to get so mad at him when he pulled your piggy tails."

"He'd make my blood boil, and then one day he just stopped and ignored me for about a year, and after that, everything was different."

"I think it's called puberty." Evelyn laughed. "And I don't remember you complaining when he started hanging around you all the time. If I remember correctly, Colt used to get jealous that he always disappeared to be with you."

"Well, he is pretty cute." Indie's eyes teared up and her mouth began to tremble. "I mean, was. Evelyn, after the funeral, it's like he's really gone." Great sobs escaped her. "I don't know if I can breathe. It's like the air has been sucked from my body."

Evelyn wrapped her arms around her like a mother would a child and stroked her hair. "I know it doesn't seem like you'll ever be okay again, and I can't promise that you'll ever stop missing him. But you have been left with a gift. A little piece of him is growing in your belly. And I know you're going to be the best mom to that child, and Misty and I, we're going to be right here with you, every step of the way." She kissed the top of her crying friend's head. "If you need us to breathe for you, then that's what we'll do."

Evelyn's heart twisted in despair for her friend, knowing just how hard the future was going to be. Colt would make sure Indie and the baby wanted for nothing. Heck, that was the benefit of having a billionaire for a brother. But Colt's money wasn't going to be able to buy the one thing Indie would always crave. As she rocked her friend, holding her in loving arms as the shuddering, messy grief poured from her, a silent tear tracked down Evelyn's face as she vowed to be strong no matter how desperately she wanted to break.

THE FUNERAL WAS HEARTBREAKINGLY poignant with a bright Texas sky that seemed too joyous for the somber occasion. Evelyn took it as a personal affront, angry that it wasn't as dark and gray as she felt inside. The good pastor had spoken of Bennett, his words tempered by the fondness he'd felt for the boy he'd watched grow into a man. Throughout the service, Indie had sat motionless between Colt and Bennett's parents except for dabbing at her damp eyes.

Evelyn sat with Logan and Misty, having had to place herself between them. Today was not the day for a petty flareup between them, although knowing how each of them had loved Bennett, she felt it was highly unlikely. Logan's younger sister, Shelby, who having been a good two years younger than the girls had always trailed after them as kids, was sitting beside Logan. Evelyn hadn't seen her for years, and the last she'd heard, Shelby had taken a job in town as an apprentice mechanic and was renting some land.

Head bowed low and with the pastor by her side, Indie shuffled to where Bennett lay in a deep walnut coffin and rested her hand against it, her shoulders shaking.

"Poor Indie," Misty murmured. "I was thinking, maybe we should stick around for a bit."

Evelyn nodded, not taking her eyes away from their grieving friend. "I was thinking the same thing. Bennett and her were never apart, and now with the baby..." Her voice trailed off. She didn't know what Colt's plans were, or if he'd even thought that far ahead. She stared at the back of his head in front of her, dark brown hair freshly combed and slicked back.

"No!" Indie's voice was shrill as she pulled her arm away from the pastor. He looked around helplessly as he once again tried to move the sobbing woman on. "No!"

Colt sighed, a world of regret captured in that single exhale, and rose slowly to his feet. He made his way over, broad shoulders stooped, and wrapped an arm around his crying sister, murmuring to her.

"I can't do it." Indie's heart shattered through the agonized words. "I can't leave him, Colt. I can't let him leave me." She buried her face into his chest, weeping. "Why did he have to leave me?" This time quieter and more gut-wrenching for the note of defeat through the pain.

Evelyn sniffled as the scene before her blurred, the vision

drowned in her own tears. She was aware of Logan sitting rigidly beside her, and it hit her with a devastating impact that the three musketeers of her youth were no more. *Goodbye, Bennett.*

~

IT FELT like a lifetime ago that Colt had made this drive with his sister, but back then it had been from their mother's funeral. The drive to the house was no longer rutted, but was sleekly asphalted, the large, powered gate at the front gleaming with the brand of the ranch. In the years since he'd taken over shared ownership, he'd spent grandly on upgrading and modernizing every aspect of the property.

Now as they pulled up to the large house that could humbly be described as a mansion—albeit of a billionaire rodeo star—he wondered what his parents would have thought about it all. He bet his father would have loved soaking in the hot tub, easing his aching old bull rider joints, or maybe the sauna. He'd added the library and wine cellar because he'd once read that it was something that wealthy people had. For himself, he'd chosen to invest in a state-of-the-art gym to help him be in the best physical condition possible for his sport. He'd turned the old place into something, that was for sure. But regardless of the improvements, he knew his parents would have loved having a grandkid or kids running about the place. Now, their ranch that he'd turned into a billionaire rancher's playground would be Indie and Bennett's child's legacy.

"I don't like thinking about him being alone." Indie's voice was raw from the power of her anguish.

"Indie, I don't rightly know if there's anything to like about this situation." Colt rubbed his forehead. "Dad, Mom, now Bennett. Sometimes I wonder if we were born under an unlucky star."

His sister looked so young in the truck beside him, too young to have lost so many. "I wonder if maybe I'm destined to be like Mom." Before he could ponder the meaning of her words, she turned her red-rimmed eyes to him. "Do you know what I put in the coffin with Bennett?" Colt shook his head. "A picture from the first ultrasound we had and a little teddy that had *I love Daddy* on its belly. I wanted him to know how much his baby loved him." Indie's voice broke.

"Indie, I have never seen Bennett prouder than when you guys told me about the baby. Well, except for that time you said you'd go to Senior Prom with him. The man strutted like a peacock for weeks."

Fresh pain knifed through Colt. It didn't seem possible that there wasn't going to be any more memories to be made with Bennett. He swallowed thickly, fighting to keep his composure, knowing Indie needed him to be strong. It was with a welcome sense of relief that Logan's old truck pulled up with Evelyn, Misty, and his kid sister, Shelby, as passengers. Memories hit him again and he battled to push them away before he embarrassed himself. Thankfully, the girls paid him little attention, quickly going to Indie and escorting their weeping friend to the porch and settling her on the swing. Hopefully they could provide her with more comfort than he'd been able to.

"I keep looking around for Bennett." Logan cleared his throat, staring off across the paddock, hands thrust deep into his pockets.

"Yeah, me too."

Logan walked back to his truck and returned with two beers, handing one over as he took a slug of his own. "Is that a new bull I see out there?"

Colt gratefully latched onto the beer and the change in

subject—one that didn't hurt so darn much. "Algebra Sucks? Yeah, he's one of Travis's."

Logan snorted. "I see Teeny's still naming all of her father's bulls for him?"

"Yeah, and soon he's gonna have a son to continue the tradition, too."

"Good for him. Are you planning on getting into the rough stock breeding business?" The men made their way over to lean on the fence rail, both mirroring the other and resting a foot on the lower rung.

The sight of all the freshly painted white fencing soothed Colt's mind. "It was something that I'd thought Bennett would do well at." Somewhere out in a field he could hear Big Wheels calling, probably to the latest mare he'd developed an attachment to.

"He might not have ever wanted to sit on them or run from one, but he sure was good at keeping them." Logan gave a chuckle. "You remember that time old Dave Warner's bull went for him? Man, I never knew Bennett could run that fast."

"Or jump that high. I swear he cleared that gate by a good foot or two." Colt couldn't help laughing aloud himself. "I told him he had a bright future ahead of him working with you as a rodeo clown."

"And he told you he already spent enough time hanging out with clowns."

"And you said you resembled that remark."

Colt took a swig from his bottle. It still hurt like all heck thinking about Bennett not standing there with them, that he never would again. But he didn't want to not think about one of the best friend's he'd ever had, or the brother-in-law he'd almost had. He glanced over his shoulder to where Indie was still huddled, surrounded by the women who refused to leave her side.

It was easy to pick Evelyn with her dark hair sitting beside her, gently swinging her legs even as she had an arm around Indie. As if sensing his gaze, she looked up and smiled sadly at him. Even from that distance, he somehow felt like she was checking on him, that she understood he was hurting too, and she wanted to make sure he was okay. A feeling of connection stretched between them until she returned her attention back to Indie, and it snapped, leaving him once again standing in a field with his best friend, mourning a man who had meant so much to all of them.

CHAPTER 5

*I*t was as if Colt permeated every aspect of Evelyn's world. Everywhere she turned, there he was. He'd be there across from her at the enormous table—Indie had once told her it was imported from Spain— in the evening when everyone gathered, laughter filling the room as the friends shared their day long into the evenings. And when the girls would sip iced tea and gently swing on the porch, she could see him going about his day, working his horses, or moving stock or a million different things that were part of life on a ranch.

Evelyn had to admit that, more than once, her gaze had strayed to him when he'd returned to the house for a quick bite to eat, his shirt clinging to his broad shoulders, damp from his exertions. And she didn't even need to start thinking about the way his jeans hung snug about his hips. It was a wonder she didn't start fanning herself in front of the others. But then again, Evelyn was used to looking at Colt like a beautiful work of art—something that she marveled she was lucky enough to admire but was definitely out of her reach. Heck, she'd been doing that since she was ten years old.

"Indie, I have some people coming to the house this afternoon and I want you to be around to meet them." Colt wiped the perspiration from his brow with the back of his hand before rubbing at his strong jawline. Evelyn thought the five o'clock shadow only added to his rugged handsomeness.

"Why? What are they coming here for?" Indie asked, looking perplexed as to why she was required.

"I'm interviewing them for the housekeeper position," Colt replied. "I figure that it might be time we have someone here to help out a bit around the house."

"Are you saying you don't like how I keep the house?" Indie's color was high, indignation flaring crimson across her cheeks.

Colt's mouth thinned. Evelyn had seen that sign of sibling annoyance many times before. She briefly entertained the concept of going inside and making another jug of sweet tea before discarding the idea. There was no need, after all, to draw attention to herself and get dragged into the argument that was brewing.

"No, but you aren't my servant. And look at you. You're pregnant. How long will it be before you can't even bend down to plug the vacuum into the wall?"

Misty and Evelyn looked at each other. *Oh no, he didn't just say that. Indie's going to—* "Are you calling me fat?" Evelyn winced at the shrillness in Indie's voice.

"No. Girls, help me out. I did not, in any way, just call her fat." Colt looked pleadingly at them.

"I plead the fifth." Misty held her hands up, clearly not willing to get involved.

"Evelyn?" Colt gave her big green puppy dog eyes.

When he looked at her like that, Evelyn swore her heart

almost turned itself over. "I don't think he actually said you were fat, Indie."

Colt smiled smugly at his sister as Indie turned betrayed eyes to Evelyn before narrowing them at her brother. "So, what were you calling me then? Cause apparently I'm no good and you need a housekeeper."

"We need a housekeeper," he corrected. "And I'm thinking of you. I read that women in your condition get morning sickness and then there's the tiredness. A housekeeper will fix snacks for you and we won't have to worry about laundry."

"You don't worry about laundry now," countered Indie tartly. "Seriously, I can't believe you keep throwing your clothes in with mine when I put a load on."

"Sharing is caring." Colt winked at her, a pleased smile tugging at the corners of his mouth when she spluttered at him.

"Fine. What time do you need me to make myself available?" Indie glared at him.

"Three-thirty." Obviously knowing that his victory could in all likelihood be short-lived, he tipped his hat to the women. "Ladies, I best be getting back to work."

Evelyn caught herself just in time before she sighed dreamily at his departing back. It didn't matter where she'd traveled. There was just something about a cowboy.

"I think getting a housekeeper is a good idea," Misty said.

"So now you're on his side." Indie rounded on her friend, her eyes wide in outrage, before she smirked mischievously. "Of course it's a good idea. I just don't want him thinking he can make all the decisions for me."

Relief made Misty look younger than her years. "And I'm on your side. Colt's got the money to pay for it. Heck, he's had the money for years. And take it from someone who knows, it's real easy to get used to being waited on." Misty gave Indie a teasing nudge with her shoulder. "Especially those mornings when the baby keeps you up."

Indie looked down at her hands, twisting the engagement ring Bennett had given her. "The thing is, I feel fine. Shouldn't I be having morning sickness or something?"

Evelyn laughed. "I can't believe you're actually complaining about not feeling sick."

Indie poked her tongue out at her. "Well, in the pregnancy books I've been reading, they all mention it. At least my boobs are tender like they say, but I didn't expect them to get lumpy."

Misty frowned. "I'm not sure lumpy boobs are normal."

"Well, I'm pregnant and I can definitely feel a lump, and it's sore when I touch it and it's never been there before."

"Maybe it could be a blocked milk duct?" Evelyn suggested, not entirely sure what was normal in pregnancy and what wasn't.

Misty was still frowning at Indie. "When's your next appointment with the doctor?" Evelyn got a sick feeling in her stomach as she picked up on Misty's vibe.

"In a couple of weeks. After they gave me the all clear after the accident, they said I didn't need to come again till my next scheduled appointment." Indie looked as though she'd begun to pick up on the energy around her. "Why?"

"I think you need to mention this lump when you go to the doctors next." Misty's tone brooked no argument.

"Yes, Mom." Indie rolled her eyes at her friend. "Seriously, is she such a nag to you?" she asked Evelyn.

"Worse. But then again, I always was her favorite," Evelyn answered. "Now, who wants more sweet tea?" She held out the empty jug, the ice cubes having melted a while ago.

Later, the sun was casting its glorious colors of rust, red, apricot and pinks as it slowly set on the horizon. Inside Evelyn could hear Misty on the phone to her business partner back in New York. It wouldn't be long before she suspected her friend would have to return to running her business empire. Evelyn was beginning to feel the creative pull again herself, her hands itching to shape molten glass. But somehow the tug to remain here at the ranch was stronger for the time being.

"Is it safe to go inside, or are you hiding out here?" Colt took a seat beside her on the porch steps.

"Safe. Indie insisted that she's making dinner tonight and has threatened us with violence if anyone sets foot in the kitchen, and Misty's doing work stuff."

Evelyn tried to ignore the flutter in her belly. He was close enough that she could feel the warmth radiating from him. That was one hot water bottle she wouldn't mind snuggling on a cold night. She breathed in his musky fragrance of livestock, sweat and something that was all his own. *If someone bottled that, they'd get rich.* Then she remembered she was already surrounded by two self-made billionaires. Evelyn might be an internationally renowned artist, but around this group, she felt like an underachiever.

"I haven't had a chance to catch up with you since..." His voice trailed off. "Well, you know. What have you been doing since we last saw each other—I think it was a couple of Christmases ago? Still busy with the glass?" He quirked a dark brow at her in question.

"Yeah, I just finished a big commission for a big name in Hollywood. Obviously, I can't disclose his name"—she gave a modest shrug—"confidentiality and all that. You understand."

"The house is big enough. You're more than welcome to find a spare room and do some work while you're here."

Evelyn laughed at his naivety, although genuinely touched that he would think to make the offer. "My apartment back home is smaller than your refrigerator. Seriously, why do you need one that big?"

"Bryce told me it was the best one to buy." Colt ruefully rubbed the back of his neck, looking sheepishly up at her.

"An appliance is an appliance. Does it matter if it's the most expensive?"

"Spending money on the ranch, that's easy to do. I know how to run it and be a cowboy. But..." He spread his hands wide. "I don't really know what to do with the money after that. It doesn't mean that much to me. I mean, I know that I never need to check price tags, but I also don't own fancy suits or a plane like Misty. I still remember the tough years with Mom and Dad. I guess maybe I like the security of knowing it's there more than spending it."

Evelyn had never really thought about it. Money had been tight for all of their families growing up and she had definitely fit the image of a struggling artist through art school and then the hard years of trying to make a name for herself. She'd seen Misty splash her money around grandiosely. The woman's closet was probably worth more than everything Evelyn owned and yet every penny she had spare was reinvested into her studio.

"Thank you for your offer to work from here, but my studio is set up in an old warehouse. With the furnaces and kilns, not to mention all the vessels and tools I need, it's not really something that can be run from a bedroom." She touched his thigh lightly. "But thanks."

"Darn, girl. I was going to offer something bigger than a bedroom. I would offer you my conference room, but Misty seems to have made herself at home in there. The library has the double height ceiling for ventilation, but I don't think a furnace would mix well with all the exposed timber and carpets. Maybe I could move some of my cars and toys out of the garage if that would suit—it's a twenty-four bay one."

"It can wait. Right now, I'm here for Indie."

The silence that stretched between them as they watched

the colors in the distance become muted was one that spoke of long acquaintance and familiarity. "You know, when you were overseas, Indie missed you so much. She was such a pain." Colt gave her a teasing side glance.

"I told her to come and visit, but she always said I sounded too busy. I mean, that wasn't true, but when I was at art school, there was all of London to explore and then, after that, the magic of Venice. I really wish she'd come and seen them with me. Maybe she could have brought you and Bennett."

"Little Evelyn Hart with the braces and ponytail. It's hard to believe all the places you've been to and seen." There was a gleam to his eye that made Evelyn's stomach do funny things. "You know, back in the day when we were younger, I had a bit of a thing for you." She could only stare at him in disbelief at his off-the-cuff comment. Her younger self had filled several diaries with teen angst over her crush on her best friend's big brother being unrequited. "But then I think I always knew you were destined for bigger things than staying in Texas as a rancher's wife."

Did he just say wife? Like he'd thought about marrying me? Evelyn kept her features composed as she smiled back at him. "I'd hardly call you just a rancher. Aren't you, like, the most eligible billionaire bachelor in the country?"

Colt rubbed the back of his neck, looking up at her ruefully. "Yeah, ever since my buddy, Bryce, up and got married, the mantle seems to have fallen to me. Anyway, you're this big fancy glass artist, famous around the world. Somehow I think you've got me beat."

"I'm sorry, did the billionaire rodeo champion who has all the women sighing over him just say I had him beat? Actually, I have to admit, that did kinda surprise me," she said with a hand on her heart.

"That I became a rodeo champ?"

"No, I could always see that happening. I just would never have picked you as being the one out of all of our friends who would end up making billions. I mean, Misty was always the brains, and I wasn't surprised when it happened to her. But you..." She left the words hanging.

Colt shrugged, a half smirk playing on his lips. "Well, I've always been able to pick my friends, and I have this one real smart one who I listen to. And when he said to invest with everything I had, I did." He gave another rueful shrug. "Who knew green energy would take off so much? And ever since then, Bryce has given me a few more helpful little tips along the way. Kinda helped keep the nest egg growing."

"And winning the various championships and endorsements along the way have helped, too.' Evelyn couldn't resist pointing it out.

"My dad always said that money attracts more money, and I guess that's kinda been true."

"Are you guys gonna sit out there all night?" Evelyn jumped. Judging from the way Colt jerked, he hadn't heard his sister come out to the porch either. "Dinner is getting cold on the table while you two jabber away out here."

Colt rose to his feet and, ever the gentleman, extended his hand to help Evelyn. If she felt a twinge of annoyance at her friend, then that was just because she didn't like being startled. *Wasn't it?*

COLT WOULD DENY it to his dying days, but there was something nice about having a houseful of women. For one, they just smelled better, and they weren't always cussing and talking things up, always trying to be the big man of the group. So far, he'd had several informative discussions with Misty about what her company was working on and what she saw as good investment opportunities. The new house-keeper, Trixie, was just what the doctor ordered, always fussing over everyone and making sure they'd had enough to eat and all the laundry she'd neatly folded smelled like sunshine. Sometimes Colt would find Indie sitting with a sad little half-smile on her face, as if she was polishing some treasured memory of Bennett in her mind. But on the whole, she smiled and laughed more each day.

And then there was Evelyn. Gorgeous, sweet Evelyn. Colt would be lying to himself if he didn't admit that, if she wasn't Indie's best friend and someone he'd known and cared about as a friend since she was a girl, well, she was someone that he'd definitely have put some moves on. But his father's words echoed in his ears—*don't poop where you eat.* There was no way Colt was going to mess up the harmonious way of life they'd all fallen into on the ranch.

Sometimes though, he'd look at Evelyn and wonder. And then he'd start to get twitchy, the urge to load up Big Wheels and get back on the road hitting him hard.

Colt gave the tractor a final wipe with the rag. Heck, he loved shiny new machinery. It would almost be a shame to get this big rig dirty. "I thought I'd find you out here." Indie walked into the barn. "Staring at your new toy, I see."

"It's a highly technical and valuable piece of machinery that will enable me to run the ranch more efficiently." Colt assumed a grandly pompous tone, his hands clasped behind his back as he lectured.

Indie giggled. For a moment she looked like a carefree teenager again, the shadows around her eyes lifting. "Whatever you say. I can tell you're starting to get a bit stir crazy being here all the time. In fact, I can't think of a single instance in years that you've been here this long."

"There are things I have to do around the ranch, and it just wouldn't feel right for me to up and go." He didn't have to say that Bennett had been the one who'd run the ranch for him or that he'd somehow always felt Indie would be okay when his friend was around.

Indie sat down on a bale of straw with a little sigh. Though she still wasn't really showing much of a belly yet, it was obviously starting to impact her standing stamina. "You don't need to stay here on account of me. Misty's going to be heading back to New York soon, but she promised to keep coming back around her work commitments. And Evelyn promised to stay as long as I need her, but she has to get back to her studio and art soon, no matter what she's telling me." Indie gave another sigh, this one infinitely sadder. "At some point I need to stand on my own two feet. You made sure I've got Trixie now to hover over me like a mother hen. I'm going to be all right. I just get a little sad sometimes when I miss Bennett, but that's okay too."

Colt's stomach clenched at the mention of his dead friend, he needed to face up to the fact that his sister was a widow now, because it was apparent she had. Indie patted her belly tenderly.

"This baby is my future, and that's what I need to focus on. My little piece of Bennett."

The quiet acceptance in his little sister's voice brought a lump to his throat. "Well, how about I stick around for a week or so longer. There are still some things I'd like to finish."

"That works out fine with me, but first there's something I need to do for me." She held her hands out for him to help her to her feet.

"Yeah? What's that?" Colt gently pulled her up.

"I want you to come to an appointment with me."

~

THE GRAY SPLODGE SQUIRMED LANGUIDLY, and for a moment Colt felt like he was intruding and then wonder infused his soul, filling him to his very core. "That's your baby, Indie." He pointed at the screen.

Indie turned her head from the bed she lay on, exposed belly covered in clear goop. "I hope so. Otherwise something has gone very wrong."

Colt peered at the screen again, trying to make out any features. "It doesn't really look like either of you."

"That just means it's determined to be its own little person. I think it's perfect." Indie looked at the ultrasound operator. "Can you tell if it's a boy or a girl?"

"I can as long as your baby cooperates. Would you like me to try?"

Indie scrunched her face in comical anticipation. "What do you say, Uncle Colt? Shall we find out if you're having a niece or a nephew?"

"Let's do it." Colt wasn't sure he had a preference. Another girl to add to his house would be nice, but a mini-Bennett would be a gift too.

"Let me just see here." The technician moved the wand about, brow furrowed in concentration. Colt didn't know how she could tell what was what. The shape on the screen looked like something he'd once made with Play-Doh in preschool. "It looks like you're having a girl."

Indie tore her shimmering eyes from the screen. "Did you hear that, Colt? Bennett and I are having a baby girl."

Colt didn't trust his voice to speak. So, smiling at his sister, he nodded instead. He prayed this little one would heal some of the pain her family had been through. A little ray of joy they could all cling to.

CHAPTER 6

*D*ust rose from the arena, buffeted by the wind as it rose into the air, twirling about like a tornado. *The barrel racers must be at it.* Colt stretched his legs out in front of him where he sat on the step of his trailer, Big Wheels dozing in the sun where he was tied up beside him. The crackle of the announcer over the loudspeaker and cheers of the crowd were music to his soul. *Man, it was good to be back on the road.* It had been one heck of a year so far, but he was beginning to find his equilibrium again.

Colt watched lazily as Logan strode over and plonked down beside him. "I thought for sure I'd find you hanging about the arena checking out all the cowgirls making their rounds."

"Yeah, Big Wheels and I are just having a moment, soaking up the sun."

Logan frowned at him. "You've changed, Colt, and I'm not sure it's for the better. Where's my wingman? The mighty Colt Montgomery, appreciator of fine cowgirls everywhere."

Colt squinted at his friend, the sun glaring despite his dark sunglasses. "He's just easing himself back into the saddle. Don't you worry, he's still in there." But Colt wasn't so sure. Somehow, he doubted any cowgirl out there could hold a candle to laughing, soft blue eyes.

"Hey, I saw Bryce and Savannah just before. He says he wants a drink with you later, but I'd say he wants to check up on you."

"He just wants to catch up for a drink cause he knows I owe him one." Colt laughed, shaking his head slowly. It was always good to see Bryce, although these days he wasn't that much of a drinker, only having one before he stopped.

"Hey, I've been meaning to ask, when you head home, will Misty be there?" Logan sucked on his cheek as he stared into the distance, an air of apparent casualness to his body.

"I'm not sure. I know Indie mentioned something about her having to start spending more time back in New York for business. Why?"

"No reason. But if she's there, I think I might head straight to my place and skip going to the ranch."

"Are you scared of her?" Colt couldn't resist teasing his friend. "I remember a time when all you wanted to do was spend time alone with her."

"I was sixteen, and she's not the same girl I knew in high school." Logan refused to look at Colt, a muscle twitching in his jaw.

"I'd say none of us are the same as back then. It's called growing up." He gave his friend a none-too-gentle nudge with his shoulder, sending Logan flying off his perch and into the dirt. "Well, at least some of us grew up. Others just switched from being the class clown to a rodeo clown."

"Rodeo Protection Athlete," Logan growled, picking himself up and dusting off the seat of his jeans.

Colt snorted. "Sorry, Rodeo Protection Athlete. Have you just tried telling her you're sorry?"

"I have nothing to be sorry for." Logan's foot began to twitch.

"Well, obviously Misty thinks you do." Colt was enjoying his friend's discomfort just a little too much.

"It's gonna be a cold day in—"

"Hi, Colt. Are we going to see you around later?" a pretty blonde cowgirl asked, waving her fingers at him. Her friends giggled behind her.

Logan spluttered at the interruption before giving her his best seductive smile. "Ladies, I will personally guarantee that Colt will put in an appearance tonight." He gave a final pat to his backside before sauntering over and draping an arm around two of the giggling cowgirls. "But to be on the safe side, it might be best if you give me all of your numbers."

Colt could only shake his head at his friend's smooth moves as he watched him walk away with the bevy of beauties. *Some things never changed.*

BIG WHEELS BACKED IN, waiting for his cue to spring forward. Colt could feel the big chestnut's muscles bunch under him like coiled springs. Every nuance the horse made and every change in the atmosphere around him barely registered on a conscious level. All his attention was focused on the calf ready to be released. *Breathe. Any minute now.* And then the animal was away. Big Wheels leaping forward broke the barrier, and with eyes trained on his quarry, Colt swung the rope and let it fly through the air and over the steer's head. Before his boots hit the sand, the horse was already backing up, taking the slack out of the rope as Colt expertly flipped the calf on its side and strung its legs together, throwing his hands up in the air to stop the clock. A quick glance up at the screen revealed the entire thing had taken under six seconds.

Taking his horse's reins up, he released the tension in the rope and freed the calf, giving his broad shoulders a wiggle to ease the muscles. If he wasn't mistaken, that time was enough to put him in the lead—and a very nice check with it. *Not bad work really.* Colt waved with his signature slow lazy smile at some female fans screaming his name and waving a sign with his name on it. *Yep, not bad work at all.*

Colt basked in the glow of returning to doing what he did best long into the evening, helped by way of lubrication of the liquor variety at the rodeo bar. Logan, the operator that he was, had indeed managed to secure the girls' numbers and now had one of them sitting on his lap. Colt wasn't sure how he'd managed it, given he was still decked out in all his rodeo clown splendor. Nonetheless, he was currently engaged in whispering sweet nothings into the cowgirl's ear as she wore his hat. Colt could only raise his glass in salute as he chuckled at the sight. His friend was in a league of his own— even if that involved a heavy dose of grease paint.

"Good to see you haven't lost your touch," a warm Texas drawl teased over the loud music and conversations.

Colt knew that voice anywhere. He looked up into the smiling face of his business partner, investment adviser, friend, and all-round nice guy. "Bryce." He reached out and shook hands with the Texan businessman. "What am I supposed to do when you've already roped the prettiest cowgirl here?" He hugged Bryce's wife, Savannah, fondly. "I see you're still putting up with this ugly old man. Just give me a sign, and I'll rescue you."

Savannah giggled, tossing her auburn hair over her shoulder. "I don't know, he has his uses. I think I might keep him around."

"Thank goodness for that." Bryce held a chair out for his

wife before pulling one from another table for himself, turning it around to straddle it. "I see you have your hands full over there, Logan."

"Yes, sir. If I keep my hands busy, maybe I'll stay out of trouble." The girl on Logan's lap gave out a squeal as he tickled her.

"Or more likely get you right into it, I'm guessing," Bryce said dryly, brow arched.

"Looks like you're aiming to defend your world championship buckle, Savannah," Colt said, nodding his head to the gold buckle at her slender waist.

"Yeah, Nova just seems to keep getting better with age. Frankie has another Delilah baby at home that she says is even better. I know Chloe's been dying to start training that one." She gazed adoringly at her husband. "But for now, Nova is more than getting the job done."

Bryce put his arm around his wife's shoulders. Colt had been wondering how long it would be before he found a reason to touch her. He'd never met a couple who needed to be touching as much as those two. He wondered what it felt like to love someone the way they obviously did. His phone vibrated in his jeans pocket, stopping that line of thought. Glancing down, Colt saw Indie's number. "Excuse me, I need to get this."

Swiftly leaving the bar, he found a quiet spot. "Hi, Indie. Yes, I won tonight." When the expected banter wasn't forthcoming from his sister, he pulled the phone away from his ear to check if they hadn't somehow gotten disconnected. "Are you still there, or just overcome with my sheer awesomeness?"

"Oh, um, that's great." There was a note in her voice that didn't sound right. "I was just wondering when you're home next."

"End of the week like we planned. Why?"

"Oh, just checking." Indie's voice was fragile and shaking.

"Indie, is everything okay? Are you crying?" Colt was becoming increasingly uneasy. "Indie?"

"I'm fine. Just tired, I guess, and missing my big brother. Knowing you, you were probably at a bar celebrating with Logan. I should let you get back to it."

Colt looked guiltily back at his friend who was whispering all sorts of promises in the cowgirl's ear. "Indie, if there's something wrong you can tell me."

"I know, Colt. But there's nothing so important that it can't wait. Oh, and congratulations on winning tonight."

"Thanks, sis. I'll see you in a week, okay?"

"Yeah, love you." Indie spoke in an odd, but gentle tone.

"Love you, too." When the line went dead, Colt stared at his phone, a sick leaden feeling settling in his stomach. His little sister was keeping something from him, and he wasn't going to wait an entire week to find out. Looks like he was heading home to the ranch.

∾

"I HAVE BREAST CANCER."

Those four little words had the power to stop his world and he could only stare at his sister in horror. "What do you mean you have breast cancer? It doesn't make any sense. How could you have cancer?" Colt's whole world shook around him, leaving him nauseous, his stomach clenching. How could this be happening again? First his father with pancreatic cancer and now his sister with breast cancer. What, were they cursed?

"I found a small lump and I thought it was something to do with my pregnancy. When I mentioned it at an appointment, they did a biopsy just to be on the safe side and it came back as cancer. Stage three."

Colt swallowed. Stage three. This wasn't his first rodeo. He knew what that meant. He couldn't sit still any longer, standing to pace the room as if it would help the turmoil rolling through his mind. "So, when do you start treatment? I'll need to arrange for a private nurse to come and stay for the duration. Obviously, we want you seeing the best doctor in the country." He paused when Indie didn't answer. "What?"

"Colt, I'm not having any treatment till after I have my baby. I won't risk her." Her face was full of strength, shining with a steadfast and serene peace.

"Indie, it's stage three. You and I both know what that means. It's not something you can mess about with and wait. You need to start now. I'm calling your doctor to make the arrangement." His voice was firm, final, not betraying a single hint of the panic lashing him.

"No, Colt. You won't call my doctor. I've made my decision and it's final. I'm not having any treatment until after the baby is born." She lifted her chin and unflinchingly met his burning gaze. "The doctor spelled it all out for me. I'm stage three, which means it's moved outside of the breast tissue. It's already in my lymph nodes. Do you know that by the time I actually found the lump, I'd already had cancer in my body for two to five years?"

"Don't be stupid, Indie. Have you even thought this through? I know the stats. With stage three, if you have treatment right away, you have a survival rate over a five-year period of roughly 72%—or that's what they told us at that breast cancer fundraising rodeo I did last year." He flung the words at her like stones, guilt only making him angrier when she flinched.

"I'm not stupid and I'm not a child. But what's an extra five years if I don't have this baby to spend it with?" Indie's nostrils flared, her face pale with fury.

"Well, then stop acting like one," Colt roared at her. Afraid at what he would say next, he stormed from the room.

When the haze of madness finally left him, he found that he'd destroyed the feed room. Buckets, grain and barrels were all overturned and strewn about the room. Outside horses moved restlessly, kicking out at their stalls, panicked at the fury erupting out of sight. Colt's legs gave way and he crumpled to the ground in despair. How could this be happening again—and to his baby sister? He'd sworn he would never let anything happen to her. The room seemed to empty of oxygen, and he struggled to draw breath in great, ragged gasps. Spots danced before his eyes, pain in his chest striking to his soul, pulling him into blackness. And then cool hands were drawing him into warm arms, a soothing voice promising they would figure it out together.

At last, he regained some semblance of composure. "She sent you." It wasn't a question.

"She asked me to talk to you. She said you might need a friend right now." Evelyn's sad gaze was indefinitely compassionate.

"You knew?" It made him feel better that Indie hadn't been going through the past week dealing with this alone.

"She told me and Misty when she found the lump, and I went with her when she had the biopsy."

"You need to make her change her mind. She won't listen to me." Even to Colt's ears, it sounded panicky.

Evelyn took his large hands in hers. He'd never noticed all the pale, silvery scars before. Some thin, others raised, all marks of lessons learned honing her craft. This woman knew what it was to hurt in the pursuit of perfection. "No, Colt, I won't. You're the one who needs to listen to her. She's made her decision as a mother and she will protect this baby, this piece of Bennett, with every fiber of her being."

"It's not fair." He couldn't lose Indie. The thought filled

him with such overwhelming blackness that his mind gibbered on the brink of insanity. "She said living another five years wouldn't be worth it without the baby, but what if she still doesn't get to spend that time with it? What if the cancer spreads more? What about her leaving us? Has she even thought about that?"

Gently, Evelyn began to rub the back of Colt's hand with her thumb, the rhythmic strokes anchoring his soul. "No, it's not fair. But what we're going to do is support Indie in this. And as soon as she has that baby, you're going to bring all your money, and I'm going to bring all my faith, and Indie, well, she's going to bring all that fight she has inside of her, and we're going to beat this thing. Indie isn't going to leave us and she sure as heck isn't going to leave that baby."

Sitting there, staring down at her strong, competent hands holding his, somehow he found the hope that together, with everyone who loved Indie, they would be able to help her fight the biggest battle of her life.

CHAPTER 7

*I*t seemed surreal to Colt that, after the initial prognosis, it was as though everyone had forgotten about Indie's cancer. Sure, it niggled away at the back of his mind that his sister had it, but to look at her glowing happy face and rapidly swelling belly, there were no outward indicators of it. Later he would look back at that time as some of his most bittersweet memories of the little family they'd made at the ranch.

Colt leaned his shoulder against the doorframe, watching as Evelyn struggled to assemble a white cot in the nursery. She blew at a stray piece of hair only to have it fall back into her face again. Frustration made her pout and she looked cute as heck.

"You need a hand?"

Evelyn looked up from the cot, laughing good-naturedly at having been caught in her battle against the furniture. Those sparkling periwinkle blue eyes did funny things to his stomach, but darn, they always did.

"Misty was meant to be helping me, but she got a call that she just *had* to take, and then Trixie came and said that she had some brownies she'd just taken out of the oven and Indie disappeared."

Colt swaggered over and held one side of the cot steady so she could secure the other with a screw. "But you just had to stay until you got the job finished."

"If you start something, you should always aim to finish it," she said tartly, giving the screw one final turn. And that right there was one of the reasons he'd never tried to fool around with her. If he made a move, he knew he'd best be making it for serious.

"I can just pay someone to do it and then we can both go down and have some of Trixie's brownies while they're still warm from the oven." Colt found himself thinking about the gooey chocolate spilling onto Evelyn's lush lips and her licking it away with her pink tongue—

Focus, Colt. It's Evelyn, for darn sake!

"No. This is for the baby, and I want to make sure it's perfect." She let go of her side of the frame. "And look, we've just finished the hardest part. I should be able to do the rest myself now."

He could only smile at the self-satisfaction that radiated off her. "I never had my doubts, but thanks for letting me feel like you needed me. Even if it was just for my rugged manly good looks." He struck some exaggerated bodybuilder poses.

"I always like having you around, Colt Montgomery. Sometimes you're even handy, and other times I just want something pretty to look at." Evelyn gave him a saucy wink.

Colt felt himself grow hot under her teasing. *Fancy calling a man pretty!* He quickly changed the subject. "I know it means a lot to Indie that you and Misty are here. I think it helps her not miss him so much." He didn't need to say Bennett's name. He still felt his presence every single day. "And I'm grateful, too."

"It's what you do for people you care about." Her tone was

matter of fact. "Now, if you're going to stand there jabbering away, best hold this other bit for me." Evelyn handed him another section of the cot like the two of them building nursery furniture was the most natural thing in the world.

"Yes, ma'am." Colt pretended to tip his hat and went to work.

⁓

COLT PAUSED ON THE THRESHOLD, rubbing his hand that had managed to get caught in the cot, finally having completed the job to Evelyn's satisfaction. "How many of those brownies have you had?" Colt asked, staring impressed at his sister as he held his own plate laden with treats.

"A wise man never asks that of a pregnant lady."

"Good thing I've never been accused of being wise then." Indie poked her tongue out at him as he sat down beside her. For a moment it felt like they were kids again and Mom had sent them outside with a plate of goodies so they wouldn't get crumbs in her clean kitchen. "Do you ever think about Mom and Dad?"

"Yeah, all the time. Sometimes I get sad that Mom isn't here. I have so many questions I want to ask her about being a mother." Indie's face was wistful as she took another bite of brownie.

"I wish I could show Dad what I did with the ranch or my gold buckles." Colt sighed, trying to release some of the heaviness in his heart. Like usual, it didn't work.

"Do you think Mom and Dad are keeping Bennett company? I don't like to think he's lonely up there." There was a sad catch to Indie's voice.

Colt gave a sad laugh. "I think so. But knowing Bennett, it wouldn't be too long before he was friends with everyone."

"Yeah, I miss him. I miss them all." Colt wrapped his arm

around his sister, and she leaned in, resting her head on his shoulder as if the weight of her grief was too much.

"Me too." He swung his legs, the rhythm soothing against the tide of sorrow. "Me too."

~

THE LARGE METAL framed windows set high in the exposed red brick wall allowed the sunlight to flood in, giving the studio in the old warehouse an airy feel and, more importantly, allowed for good ventilation when Evelyn needed to work. She'd been incredibly lucky to find the space available for rent. There was only so long that she would be able to not work and she'd finally bitten the bullet and committed to getting a space for herself in town. Her temporary stay was beginning to look like it might become more permanent.

The roar of the furnace set her blood to bubbling in anticipation of creation as she walked over to where her glass rods were still in their boxes, sorted by color. Her sketch pad was filled with designs that she would need to start work on. But first, she had something much more personal to do. Her hand hovered over each box as she pictured Indie in her mind, stopping at the light violet. Evelyn picked up the transparent rod and held it to the light, feeling the energy flowing through it, joyous, light. *Perfect for Indie.*

She repeated it for each of the others. Primrose yellow for the hope that the baby represented for the future, bold carmine for Misty. Evelyn had shed a tear when sturdy, strong ultramarine had revealed itself for Bennett. Opaque turquoise had called to her when she'd thought of her own spirit, and now her thoughts turned to Colt. She bit her lip indecisively. She'd never tried to channel his energy before. She closed her eyes and pictured Colt, the square jawline, soulful emerald green eyes, the strong straight nose and sensual mouth. *Maybe I need to crack the windows open wider. It's starting to feel a bit hot in here.* Evelyn fanned herself and tried to focus on the essence of the man, loyal, strong, kind, determined. Feeling a pull, she let her hand follow it and opened her eyes. Topaz, perfect. Humming softly to herself, she set to work.

She watched the glass turn malleable like toffee as she heated it and then she filled her lungs to capacity and, with control stemming from long practice, blew, deftly selecting a tool to pull and pinch and twist. Her mind soared. In this moment there was nothing but the heat, the colors and the glass. There was no grief or anguish, no fear for what would happen next, no loss. Just the joy of creation.

Later, her hair plastered to her scalp with sweat and her clothes dripping, she set the last piece into the kiln. Now that the spell had been broken, exhaustion turned her limbs leaden but, as was usual when she created, her heart was light. If only glass could fix everything so easily. But it was a fickle mistress. One misstep and it was prone to shatter, just like the heart.

THE BALMY, evening breeze was gentle as it tickled the hair on the nape of Evelyn's neck. Sitting on the porch swing with her friends, she could hear the chirps of the crickets in the fields and, once or twice, the hoot of a barn owl. A smattering of stars twinkled down at them, unfazed about what tiny humans did in what was a blink of an eye for the celestial bodies.

"William's starting to complain that he has to handle all the difficult clients while I'm gone. Do you know he actually said that I seem to magically disappear back to the ranch when I know we're having meetings with certain clients?" Misty shook her head laughing. "It's like he knows me."

"Misty, I don't want you to get in trouble with William." Indie's hand rested comfortably on her bulging belly. "I'm not due quite yet."

"I know, and I'll be heading back for a few days next week. I need to catch up with Chora about a charity ball that we need to start planning for next year." Misty rolled her eyes as she shook her head. "William is perfectly capable of looking after them, he just doesn't want to. What he forgets is I don't like dealing with them any better than he does."

"Speaking of not having to deal with someone, did I actually see Logan creeping alongside the house after visiting Colt this afternoon?" Evelyn asked, her brows sky high in disbelief. "He looked like a cat burglar from one of those old films." She mimed him pressed up against the wall, scanning the vicinity.

Indie threw back her head and let out a great peal of laughter. "Yep." She pointed a finger at Misty. "And that's the reason why."

"Hey, I didn't even know he was here." Misty scrunched up her face in fierce denial.

"But he knew you were here." Evelyn laughed.

"Well, it's good that he's scared of me. He'll think twice before he tries to fool me again," Misty declared, eyes narrowed. Evelyn privately thought that she sounded a little hurt for all her bravado.

"Well, at this rate, the poor man isn't even game to get close to you. What exactly did you say to him?" Indie asked.

"I don't think it's what I said to him, but that when he looks at me, he feels guilty. And rather than be a man and apologize, he decided to just avoid me altogether."

Evelyn rolled her eyes. "Yep, sounds like Logan."

The girls grew quiet again, nothing but the night animals

and the creak of the swing filling the void. Indie reached out and took the other girls' hands. "I love you guys."

Evelyn gave her friend's hand a squeeze for a moment, the lump in her throat making it impossible for her to respond. She swallowed it down, blinking back tears. "We love you, too." Overhead, the stars continued to twinkle.

~

THE LIGHT CAUGHT the mobile as Evelyn carefully hung it from the ceiling above the cot, sending a kaleidoscope of colors dancing on the opposite wall. A rainbow flower hung upside down, and from each carefully crafted petal, a delicate drop was suspended to represent each family member. In the very center was a bright yellow hummingbird caught mid-flight as it sipped on the nectar.

"Oh, Evelyn, it's beautiful," breathed Indie, holding her hand to her heart in awe. "Every time she looks at it, she'll feel the love we all have for her."

"I like that I'm red." Misty nodded in approval. "Makes me seem powerful."

"You are powerful," Indie retorted. "I'm delicate."

"Joyous," Evelyn corrected, stepping away from her installation. She'd done a lot of high-profile pieces in her career so far, but this one was up there as a favorite. Every creation she did was a piece of her soul, but this one was personal. It was family.

Indie gave a sharp intake of breath, her hand on her back. Misty frowned, her go-to setting when she was concerned. "Are you okay?"

"I don't know, I just got a pain in my back. Owww." Indie's hands flew to her belly.

"Is it time?" asked Evelyn. Uncertain, she glanced at Misty for guidance.

"I don't know, I've never done this before." There was a slight edge of hysteria to Indie's voice. "I was hoping one of you two would have read up on this by now."

Evelyn's stomach churned, half in anticipation, half in dread. "Maybe we should call the hospital and find out if we should head in?"

"No, she needs to be having regular contractions before that." Misty smiled encouragingly to her pale, anxious friend. "How about I run a bath for you. I *read* that it will help with some of the pains in the initial stages of labor."

"Hang on, what? This is just an ache? If it is, I don't think I can do this." No longer was it an edge in Indie's voice, but full-blown hysteria.

"You're made of tough stuff, and we're going to be here every step of the way," Evelyn soothed, going over to hold her arm reassuringly. "Now, Misty's going to get that bath ready for you, and I'm going to go find Colt and tell him what's happening."

Indie bit down on her lip to stop a moan escaping her as she bravely nodded. "If Bennett wasn't already dead, I'd kill him myself for putting me in this situation."

As Evelyn dashed from the room, she didn't know whether to laugh or correct her friend for bringing poor Bennett into it.

IT STILL DIDN'T QUITE SEEM real to Colt that his baby sister was a new mom. Indie had an expression that he'd never seen before on her face as she gazed down at her daughter. A love so pure that for a moment he felt left out, a person on the outside looking in.

"She's perfect, isn't she?" she said adoringly.

Between the blanket she was swaddled in and the little

cap on her head, all Colt could see was a squashed little nose and puffy eyes in a plump, red face. "You did real good, Indie."

And he meant that. He'd never been prouder of his sister in his entire life. The way she'd bore up under the pain that had lasted hours—and he knew, since he'd spent a fair bit of it pacing, only leaving the room when bits of his sister he didn't really want imprinted in his memory had been required to be exposed. Misty and Evelyn had never left her side once, wiping her forehead with a damp cloth, offering ice chips and rubbing her back. Toward the end, as Colt had paced outside, her exhausted moans had torn at his heart and sent him silently cursing Bennett.

Colt had called Bennett's parents to let them know their granddaughter had been born. Already old, since their son's death, they'd become shadows of their former selves, frail and empty. Even the joyous news he had for them was barely able to rouse them from it. He'd hung up the phone feeling unbearably sad at what the Gray's lives had become.

A nurse bustled in and offered Indie a bottle for the baby. Smiling her thanks, the new mom shifted her baby in her arms and the newborn lustily sucked on the teat. "Do you think Bennett would have liked her name? We never got a chance to talk about it." Sadness tempered Indie's glow.

"I think Hope is perfect, and Bennett would have love it, too. Anyway, she would have been his little princess before you could count to ten."

Indie let out a long sigh of contentment. "And I would have loved every minute of it." She bent forward and planted a tender kiss on her daughter's head, pausing to breathe deeply. "I never believed them, but newborns have the most amazing smell." There was a tinge of wonder in her voice as she looked up at him, eyes glowing. "Would you like to have a hold?"

Colt looked down at his big, work-roughened hands—hands that had helped birth calves and mend fences and now shook at the thought of holding his fragile little niece. "If you think I won't break her."

"You won't break her. Now, come over here. Hope, my love, your uncle, Colt, is going to hold you for a while." She stifled a yawn. "Mommy is just going to have a little rest. You wore me out today." Tenderly, she transferred the baby into Colt's arms.

The baby stared at him around the bottle she still sucked on. Colt didn't think Hope looked like either of her parents yet. Maybe she was always going to look like her own person. "Hi, I'm your uncle, Colt, and your mommy is my little sister and I love her very much. And your daddy, he is —" Colt's voice choked. Tonight he felt Bennett's loss keenly. "He was my best friend, so I guess you and I should probably get to know each other." A soft snore sounded from the bed. Colt looked up, a smile tugging at his lips when he saw Indie had drifted off to sleep. "All I know is your mommy loves you very much and you're so very lucky to be her daughter." He gazed back at his niece. "And I'm so very lucky to be her brother." Jiggling with each step, he considered when he'd last told Indie that. Maybe it was time he started making it a priority.

CHAPTER 8

*I*ndie's hand was cold in his, the smell of the waiting room outside of the oncologist suite bringing back memories of his dad's treatments. "Thanks for coming with me." Her voice had a tremor as she bravely gave his hand a squeeze. "Evelyn offered, but Hope will settle easily for her and I just"—Indie swallowed—"I just really needed my big brother here today."

Colt felt a burning at the back of his throat. There was no way he was going to let his sister go through this without him, even if he was terrified inside. His stomach churned like a stormy ocean, making it hard to keep his expression upbeat. Down the hall he could hear someone being vigorously ill. He shuddered, dreading when it would be Indie's turn. Desperately, he clutched on to the thought of Evelyn sitting on a blanket back home at the ranch, Hope lying on her tummy making little noises as she was fussed over. Strangely, the ocean calmed.

"Indie, I'm here no matter what." Colt was surprised at how strong and reassuring he sounded. *Maybe I can do this after all.*

"Indie Montgomery?" An efficient nurse called from the doorway.

"Yes, ma'am."

"If you would like to come with me." The nurse half turned, waiting expectantly. Indie stoically rose. Colt could feel her take in a deep breath, bracing herself. He awkwardly stood, waiting for some signal from her that she was ready. After a little nod to herself, Indie began to follow.

A silver-haired gentleman held out his hand from where he was stationed behind an immaculate desk. "Hello, Indie, it's nice to see you again." After a handshake and reassuring pat to Indie's hand, he turned kind eyes to Colt. "I see you've brought a support person today." The doctor offered his hand to Colt. "I'm Doctor Fitzpatrick."

Colt took it, noting the firm grip approvingly. There was something about this kindly, grizzled man that he found immensely reassuring. Hope sprung refreshed through him. *Everything is going to be okay. Indie's going to get some treatment, and then life will get back to normal.*

Doctor Fitzgerald consulted his notes. "I see that you've already had your blood tests and today your chemotherapy will be administered via IV. Now, I'm going to quickly take your blood pressure and a few other vitals and answer any questions you might have, and then I'll hand you over to the nurse to start your treatment."

"I read the pamphlet that Indie brought home and it mentioned the side effects. Would it be worthwhile for me to hire a nurse to help?" Colt got straight down to business, sitting straighter in his chair as the doctor wheeled over a monitor on a stand and began to put the pressure cuff on his sister. Details, that's what would help them all get through this.

"Home nurses can be quite expensive and out of the range of a lot of patients. Indie has mentioned that she is well supported at home by you and her friends," Doctor Fitzpatrick began carefully.

"Money isn't an issue for me," Colt said, cutting him off. "It's why we came to you, and I want to make sure Indie has the best care possible."

"If money isn't an issue, then it can help, even just for peace of mind. If you do decide to hire one, going forward we can fit Indie with a port and have the chemo administered via a pump. It would mean that she would be able to come here for the pump to be fitted at each treatment and then go home again rather than staying."

Colt raised his brows, impressed that there was an option that meant Indie would potentially spend less time in this challenging environment and more time at home on the ranch where she belonged with her baby. He turned to his sister. "What do you think?"

She tilted her head while the doctor took her temperature. "I think I want to get through today and then I'll worry about that tomorrow, maybe even the day after."

Doctor Fitzpatrick smiled his approval. "One day at a time, that's best. Do you have any other questions?"

Indie shook her head. "We saw what Dad went through with his cancer, so I kinda know what to expect."

"That's right, your father had pancreatic cancer I believe." The doctor wheeled his monitor back to the other side of the room.

"He did, sir," Colt said, a tightening band building around his lungs.

"Well, if you don't have any more questions, I'll hand you over to the nurse and she'll take you into the treatment room."

Colt wanted desperately to think of more questions, anything that was going to delay the inevitable. Indie thrust her chin out, gripping the armrests of her chair as she pushed to her feet. *Gosh darn, but she was the bravest person he'd ever seen.* Knowing he could do no less, he too took to his feet and followed her as she marched, head held high, to what would be her new reality for the next little bit.

THE FALLOUT from Indie's treatments were brutal. Evelyn was eternally grateful that Colt had had the good sense to hire Nurse Ingre. The kindly practical woman was a godsend. When Evelyn found herself overwhelmed with how to best help her friend, the nurse was always there, as if a sixth sense told her she was needed, to help hold hair back from her patient's face as she vomited and to wipe her forehead with a cool cloth. In those instances, Evelyn would take Hope and step outside for a moment of fresh air, to breathe in and find her inner strength to plaster a smile back on her face and return to Indie's side. This was just a hiccup, a bump in the road. Indie was a fighter and she'd beat this. Evelyn believed it to her very core. She had to. The alternative was something she couldn't process.

The smell of vomit lingered in the air as Evelyn returned to Indie's room. Nurse Ingre was constantly removing it, but even the air freshener wasn't enough to completely mask it. Indie lay pale and exhausted on the bed but valiantly raised a smile and held her arms out for her daughter when she saw them enter.

"Have you been keeping Auntie Evelyn busy?" the mother crooned.

"She knows all she has to do is give me a gummy smile and I'm lost." Evelyn rolled her eyes. "I'm a sucker."

Hope began to nuzzle at her mother's breasts, the young woman's chalky complexion going, if possible, even paler.

"Here." Indie looked away as she held the baby out. "She's hungry."

Evelyn's heart broke for her friend when she saw the glitter of tears in her eyes. "How about I go get a bottle and you feed her, just like any mom would?" She hoped that she could ease Indie's pain.

"But I'm not just any mom, am I?" Indie hit out at her breast. "What good are these things if I can't feed my baby like I'm meant to?" Fat tears began to roll down her cheeks. "I'm so angry at my body. It feels like it's turned against me and I hate it." She reached a hand up to her hair and pulled great clumps of it out, more left behind on her pillow. "Some days I'm glad Bennett is dead so he doesn't have to see me like this."

"You don't mean that." Evelyn took Hope who had begun to cry, picking up on her mother's despair. "You would give anything to have Bennett back and he would've told you how beautiful you were to him." She gave her friend's shoulder a squeeze. "And he would have meant every single word of it, too." Evelyn handed Hope back to her mother. "Now, you hold your baby, and I'll go get some formula for her."

On her way back, she could hear little coos from Hope and giggles from Indie. Feeling like an intruder, she paused at the door, leaning her shoulder against the frame to watch her friend plant kisses on Hope's tiny feet as she kicked them about to escape the tickling. In that moment, Indie had color to her washed-out cheeks and her eyes sparkled with life, not the shimmer of tears and pain. Her friend had come back.

"Formula delivery service," Evelyn announced, waving the bottle in the air.

Hope watched her with solemn eyes as she very seriously tried to fit her entire fist into her mouth. "I think someone's hungry." Indie stared down at her daughter, the love she felt clearly evident in her gaze.

"That one's always hungry. Must take after Uncle Colt."

A ball of anxiety settled in her stomach. Poor Colt, trying to hold everything together, desperately trying to not give into his fears and be there for his sister. Evelyn wasn't sure how much longer he was going to be able to carry the burden. Sure, she could be there as a friend for him, but she wistfully wondered what it would be like to be more than that, to hold him in the dark when he cried out his fears.

"I have a favor to ask," Indie said, dark smudges under her eyes.

"Anything."

"Remember the last time you said that?"

Evelyn giggled. "How was I to know you and Misty were going to gang up on me? I mean, who tries to break their car out of city lockup, for goodness sake." She laughed. "I still don't know what you thought I would do."

"Well, Misty had a plan, but you didn't want to listen to it. All you had to do was put on the wig and grab the steak—"

"Hold up, that's the bit that scared me, the steak. Why did I need a steak?"

"Well, you know"—Indie shrugged, wiping a tear of mirth from her eye—"just in case there was a dog there."

"I'm so glad Bennett overheard your plan and just paid to get your car back."

"Yeah. Evelyn, can you go out into the barn and get the clippers for me? I think Colt has them in the tack room."

"Hey, guys, sorry I'm late." Misty sauntered into the room, effortlessly chic. "There was a backlog of flights leaving and my pilot and I sat on the tarmac for what felt like ages."

"Well, you're here now. Do you want to keep our bossy friend here company while I hunt down clippers for her?" Evelyn pretended to give Indie a salute.

Misty's face scrunched up, her eyes baffled as she looked

questioningly at her friend in bed. "What do you want clippers for?"

"Just wait and see." Indie gave her a mysterious smile, the baby having fallen asleep, the teat of the bottle resting on the bottom lip of her rosebud mouth.

Hope was still sleeping when Indie ran a hand experimentally through her hair, a tentative smile playing on her lips. "What do you guys think?"

Evelyn stared in speechless awe at her friend. Her hair was now closely clipped to her scalp, emphasizing her delicate features and making her shadowed eyes huge in her gaunt face. Indie had taken back her power, wresting it from the jaws of her disease.

"You look like a warrior," Misty whispered, her expression humble in the face of such strength.

"Then I guess it's time I start acting like one." Indie retrieved her baby from Evelyn's arms. "Now, who wants to play poker?"

"The last time we played, I lost," Misty complained.

"Well, you're the one who wanted to bet on going for a skinny dip with Logan." Evelyn laughed at Misty's disgruntled expression.

"And let's call a spade a spade. The last time you lost anything was when we were all sixteen years old. That's how long it's been since you last played poker with me." Indie shook her head in mocking disbelief at her friend. She pointed to her bedside table. "The cards are in there. Start shuffling."

CHAPTER 9

*D*ays jumbled into each other, and if Colt had prayed that he would get used to the new norm of seeing his sister pale and shaky as she fought her way through each round of treatment, he was sadly mistaken. Each time it stabbed at him as if he were replaying the trauma of failing her on a constant loop. He wanted nothing more than to be a child again, back before his dad got sick. Back then, it had been so easy to pull the covers over his head and all the scary monsters in the dark would disappear.

"Excuse me, Colt, may I interrupt you for a moment?" Trixie popped her head into the conference room, obviously having been waiting outside for his video link-up with Bryce to finish. Colt's mind was still reeling with the figures and flow charts his business partner had thrown at him. The housekeeper had been a godsend, fussing over Indie and generally mothering all of them—something that the siblings hadn't experienced for a long time.

"Please come in, Trixie. I'm done now." He beckoned her with one hand as he began to gather up his things. Misty had requested the room after he'd finished. Colt gave a rueful smile. Not every mansion had a conference room, but this one was in high demand by the two billionaires under the same roof.

"Colt, I was reading an article about how a diet high in vitamin C may help cancer patients. Would you mind if I start sourcing some ingredients and trial it along with supplements? The reason I'm asking is it has a list of items that are highest in vitamin C and it recommends using them fresh. It's out of season for some of them and others, well, I have never heard of before."

"I don't see how it would hurt. Give me the list and I'll send for them. Heck, while I'm at it, we might even send for some pastries from Paris. That might get Indie eating something. I know it would help my appetite." He smiled at the kindly woman. "Indie and I appreciate everything you're doing."

"That girl in there is one heck of a fighter, and I've grown fond of her." Worry shadowed Trixie's eyes, amplified by the lenses of her glasses. "I'll fight right alongside her every step of the way to make her better, too. That baby needs her mama around," she said with an easy defiance, twisting her apron in her hands.

Colt found himself buoyed by the woman's resolve. With all of them standing with Indie, his sister was going to make it out the other side. A message flickered on the giant glossy black screen set into the wall at the end of the table. William Irvine was requesting a video meeting with Misty Monroe. Colt clicked to accept, and the urbane features of Misty's business partner appeared on screen. "Hello, William. I believe Misty is on her way down as we speak."

"Are you attending the meeting today?" William glanced down at his tablet, bafflement plain in his fussy movements.

"No, I'm just finishing up a meeting of my own. As soon as Misty shows up, I'll be out of your hair faster than you can spit," Colt drawled. He always felt the need to become more cowboy whenever he was with polished businessmen, and the well-groomed New Yorker sent the urge into overdrive. Colt might be a billionaire, but he was a cowboy first and foremost.

"Colt, William, I'm so sorry I'm late." Misty burst into the room, a cloth still draped over her shoulder from where she'd obviously been tending to the baby. Colt wondered where Evelyn was since she was the one who spent the most time with Hope. It was actually kind of cute the way they were with each other. One day she was going to make one heck of a mother. For some reason the thought of Evelyn rocking a baby in her arms while a strange man proudly smiled down at them didn't sit well with him.

He rose, Trixie having already discreetly left the room. "I'll leave you kids to it." From the narrowing of William's eyes on the big screen, the man hadn't failed to catch his patronizing tone. With zero care given to the other man's reaction, Colt swaggered from the room and headed to the kitchen. Acting cowboy always gave him the munchies.

Evelyn was propped up on a stool at the breakfast bar, tucking into a hefty sandwich. Even when she was a kid, she'd seemed to pack away a heck of a lot more food than her frame suggested. Obviously, not much had changed. Her mouth curved into an unconscious smile, her eyes sparkling over her lunch. "Would you like me to make one for you?" she offered.

"No, ma'am." He found himself smiling in reply. For some reason he'd never been able to not smile or laugh with her. "I think I can manage to wrangle some lunch for myself."

"How was your meeting?" she asked around a mouthful of food.

"It was the same as it always is. Bryce throws numbers at me, and I ask what he's planning on doing and then I tell him that I'll do the same." Colt pulled open the refrigerator. He had to hand it to Trixie, she really did have it well stocked. Maybe he should have gotten a housekeeper years ago.

"Surely it's not as bad as that." Evelyn had a smudge of butter on the end of her nose. Without thinking, he walked over and gently wiped it off with the tip of his finger. Her blue eyes were wide as she watched him, shivering slightly at his touch. Colt was intensely aware of their skin touching, his fingers tingling from the contract. Blinking, he forcibly reminded himself that it was only a mundane action. Heck, he couldn't let her spend the rest of the day with butter on her nose. No sirree. He'd done only what any self-respecting gentleman would do.

Evelyn's hand went to where he'd just touched her, a slow creep of color washing over her cheekbones. "Did I have something there?"

"Yep, but it's taken care of now." Colt tried for a light tone, anything to ease the sudden pounding of his heart, but wasn't sure he'd succeeded.

He was being silly. Evelyn Hart had been around for most of his life and had always been a good friend to Indie and to him. Why was he suddenly acting like things had changed? Heck, is this what happened when he stayed home too much? Did he suddenly forget he was a carefree billionaire cowboy bachelor with nothing to worry about but the next rodeo and which cute cowgirl was going to keep him company?

And then what Indie was going through clawed him out of his playful mood. What kind of a jerk thought about girls and not worrying about anything when, at this very moment, his kid sister was lying upstairs trying to get through the side effects of chemo? Heck, and being a new mom. Colt's misery became a steel weight in his gut.

"Are you okay?" Evelyn's soft voice broke through his guilt.

"Yeah, I just remembered there was something I need to do." He spun on his heel.

"Aren't you going to get something to eat?"

"Ah, I'll grab something later." Later, Colt would tell himself he made a dignified exit. In reality, Evelyn watched in open-mouthed surprise as he bolted from the room like hounds were on his heels.

~

HANDS ON HIPS, Evelyn surveyed her temporary studio, a faint feeling of disorientation coursing through her. It was doing the job for now, but it wasn't the space she'd spent so much time creating back home. It sure would be good to go back to her normal routine when Indie got better. In fact, her agent had been on the phone again today, pushing her to lock in a date for a new exhibition that she wanted held in London.

She brightened. Maybe everyone could come over for it. Misty, Indie and the baby … Colt. The more she thought about it, the more Evelyn liked the idea. They could all go over on Misty's private plane and then stay somewhere fancy. Make a real occasion out of it and celebrate Indie getting better. Still musing about all the possibilities the exhibition presented, she walked over to the furnace, reaching into the crucible filled with clear melted glass with her blow pipe, gathering a layer of molten glass on the end of the steel. Extracting it, she quickly made her way to the steel table, rolling the molten glass, a cylindrical shape beginning to form.

Her mind wandered again to Colt. There was no denying how attracted she was to him. *Let's face it, I'm head over heels in love with him.* Her schoolgirl crush had matured, but the timing was all wrong. Heck, she didn't even know if he would ever see her as anything more than a friend.

Evelyn blew through the pipe, her cheeks puffing out with the controlled exertions before walking it back to the furnace, the hot blast of heat baking the sweat from her brow, her eyes sandpaper dry. It was a relief to walk away from the hellish glow back to her bench and she grabbed a set of metal tongs on the way. Colt once again nudged himself back into her thoughts. Maybe she should just be satisfied with being in the friendzone. It's not like he'd ever lacked female company, and he still hadn't settled down even for a short while, let alone got serious with anyone. *Maybe, when Indie gets better, I'll make it clear that I like him. Maybe even at the exhibition.*

Images of romantic dinners in quaint English pubs and walks in leafy parks filtered through her mind. Impatiently, she pulled her drifting thoughts back together, shaking her head. *Who am I kidding? It's been years and I still haven't said anything to him.* Setting to work, she molded the malleable glass, wishing her feelings could be so easily shaped.

CHAPTER 10

"I don't understand." Colt's mind was a jumble, the words the doctor had uttered gibberish to him. Beside him, Indie had a chalky pallor to her complexion— unnaturally so. Utterly frozen, she could have been a waxed mannequin.

"I'm sorry, I wish I had better news. But the cancer has spread to your lungs, brain and bones." Doctor Fitzpatrick cleared his throat, offering a box of tissues to Indie. A single lonely tear tracked down her porcelain features. Colt felt like he was watching it happen in a movie, a passenger to the events that were unfolding.

"How long?" Indie's voice was hoarse, the words strained. The only movement was her eyes holding the doctor's gaze. "How long do I have?"

The doctor returned her look regretfully. "The statistic for stage four cancer isn't the best. The average life span is six months with a 22% survival rate."

"But there are things we can do, right, Doc?" Colt finally pushed through the numbness. "How did this even happen? Indie did everything you told her to do." With the numbness fading, a leaden weight threatened to pull him down, making it hard to breathe.

"She did, but with the treatment being delayed, it had spread further than we'd anticipated. At this stage, we can't cure it. We can try and shrink it down, but you'll always live with cancer, I'm sorry to say." Colt thought he was going to throttle the man if he was sorry for one more thing. All he needed to do was fix his sister.

"I see." A world of emotions was behind those simple words. Indie's bottom lip trembled. "What can I expect?"

"It's different for everyone, but because it has spread to your bones, there will be discomfort that will eventually become worse. I'll prescribe pain relief, and your nurse will monitor it as you need it. We will continue with the chemo and also hormone therapy. We may have to switch drugs around as they become less effective." Doctor Fitzgerald stood and came around to stand beside Indie. "I promise you won't do this alone, and I will do everything in my power to help you fight this." He gave her shoulder a sympathetic squeeze.

"Well, so far, your best hasn't been good enough," snarled Colt, his chair flying backwards as he stood.

"Colt!" Indie sounded horrified. *Typical Indie.* She'd just been handed a death sentence and all she cared about were his manners.

"It's true." Doctor Fitzgerald returned his hostile glare unflinchingly, the pity Colt saw there only stoking the flames of his anger further. "You'll have to excuse me, but I've got better things to do than listen to someone who doesn't know what they're doing." He didn't even bother to stay for Indie's embarrassed apology. He needed to find how to cure his sister.

Frigid silence had accompanied them home from the hospital. He'd tried to talk to Indie, make her see that they needed a better doctor, a better hospital, somewhere with the latest research and technology. Finally, she'd held up a hand to silence him. "I can't deal with this right now." Indie gulped hard and turned glistening eyes to him. "I need you to be whatever I need you to be, and right now, I don't need someone to fix this. I need my big brother." Her voice choked. "I need you to hold me and tell me that you love me and that I won't do this alone."

Colt pulled his truck over to the side of the road, gravel crunching under his tires as he braked sharply. He undid his seatbelt and reached over to wrap his arms around his sobbing sister. "I love you, Indie, and you better believe I'm doing this with you. You know the promise I made you when we were kids. You and me always." As his shirt became wet with her tears, he wondered if he could survive it if his promise was broken.

Six months? Colt wouldn't accept that that was all the time Indie's so-called doctor had granted her left to live. They hadn't come up against the likes of him. He was a darn billionaire, and there was no way he was going to play by their rules. Colt was going to make the rules up to suit himself and cure his sister in the process. He gathered up the information he'd printed off and went in search of Trixie. She was the first step in his plan.

"Each dish needs to have at least four of these ingredients in them and I want a constant supply of these fruits for her." Colt and Trixie both had their attention firmly focused on the piece of paper in his hand.

"This is going to be challenging." Trixie pursed her lips, her eyes narrowed as she considered the request. "Some of them—garlic, bell peppers, tomato, broccoli and snow peas—will be easy enough, but kale, papaya … what is this black cohosh? I've never heard of that before."

"No, just the ingredients below the line. Everything above it, I think, will be easier to give as supplements."

"What's going on here?" Evelyn was abuzz with curiosity, only heightened when Colt jumped in surprise.

"I was reading some papers that said certain foods could help with halting the spread of cancer. Things high in vitamin C for example, which Trixie already does, but other things like flaxseed, green tea, turmeric. I think it's worth trying. There's also hypnosis, acupuncture and aromatherapy."

The way he looked at her, like he desperately needed to hear that what he was doing was the right thing, that every-thing would be all right, made Evelyn want to hug him tight. Instead, she considered his idea. "I think that anything you try should probably be run past her doctor first."

The floorboards beneath Colt's feet suddenly seemed to be of great interest to him. "Yeah, well."

Evelyn pinned him with a level gaze. "*Yeah, well*, what, Colt?"

"I might have fired him," he muttered, a slow creep of red crawling up his neck.

"That's impossible."

"Um, I think I need to go and do some laundry." Trixie gave a shake of her head, as if to two misbehaving children as she left the room.

"Well, he doesn't know what he's doing." Colt mulishly thrust out his jaw.

"He's Indie's doctor, not yours. You can't fire him, only

she can, and I believe you'll find that he is still very much her doctor."

"He isn't making her better. She's terminal." The pain buried in those words cut through her.

"She's stage four. That means she can't be cured, but with treatment, it is possible that she can live with cancer."

"Live with it!" Colt erupted, throwing his papers across the kitchen floor. Despite his anger, they drifted gracefully downwards. "How do you live with cancer?"

"With grace and a lot of faith."

"Yeah, well I think I'm just about all out of faith." His face twisted into a mask of rage and anguish.

Evelyn reached out as if to sooth a wounded animal. "But Indie isn't. It's all she's holding on to. That and her baby. You need to support her in whatever she decides to do."

"What if I can't?" His eyes pleaded with her, begged her to somehow make this right.

"Then you need to fake it." *We all do.*

❧

EVELYN WATCHED her friend rapidly disappear in front of her eyes. The cancer spreading caused walking to become painful and Indie was bedridden, the medication no longer bringing her relief. Even blessed sleep no longer sheltered her in its embrace, insomnia now dogging her between bouts of nausea, vomiting and diarrhea. Indie complained of dizziness and she no longer felt confident to hold Hope without the aid of someone else. The baby, having just turned three months old, was nonetheless constantly in the room where her mother could see her.

Nurse Ingre was invaluable with efficiently cleaning up, administering medication and, when needed, being a shoulder to cry on. Trixie hovered, always with a cheery smile and kind word, but Evelyn had found her more than once quietly crying in the pantry when the housekeeper thought no one was around. Misty had taking up chewing gum constantly—Evelyn was amazed she didn't suffer from cramps in her jaw. The chewing only got worse when Logan would drop in.

And then there was Colt. The man was holding it together, but how long he could use his anger as a glue was anyone's guess. Right now, as she calmed the fussing baby with Misty chewing gum beside her, she could hear his raised voice in the next room.

"I don't understand why you're being so stubborn."

"I'm not being stubborn, I'm being realistic." Indie's voice wheezed. These days, she was always short of breath.

"This hospital in Germany is doing cutting edge research in stem cells. This could be the answer we're looking for." Frustration made the words harsher than Evelyn knew he meant them to be, fear giving them a razor-sharp edge.

"Colt, look at me." A pause. "I mean really look at me."

"I am."

"What do you see? Because I know what I feel. I asked Doctor Fitzpatrick to stop treatment two weeks ago."

"Why, Indie?" A tortured cry tore out of him. Evelyn closed her eyes against the pain and rocked the baby tightly against her chest. Misty had stopped chewing.

"Because I'm tired. Each day I feel myself fade away more, and I want to spend what time I have left with Hope and you and my friends. I just want to be left alone to simply be."

"I never thought you were a quitter." The words were hard and hateful.

"Colt—" Indie called, tears choking what little breath she could manage. Evelyn saw the shadow of Colt rush pass the door to the nursery.

"Do you think it's safe to go in now?" asked Misty, resuming her attack on the gum in her mouth.

"I swear I've seen cattle in the fields chew less than you do these days." Evelyn stood, her limbs leaden.

"Well, I gave up smoking recently."

Evelyn looked at her friend in surprise. "When did you start?"

"When Bennett died."

"Oh." Before Bennett had died was the last time anything had felt remotely normal. Evelyn kept hoping that, when she went to bed, she would wake up and this had all been an ugly dream. The chemical stench of Indie's room assaulted her nostrils. Nurse Ingre had only finished cleaning up moments before Colt had arrived. Against the raised bed, Indie seemed to disappear into the pillows, her collarbones sharp. Even with her sunken eyes closed, there was no hiding the deep purple shadows beneath. Her frail friend wasn't living with cancer. She was dying from it.

"Maybe we should come back," Misty whispered.

"No, stay with me." Indie opened her eyes and, when she spied her daughter in Evelyn's arms, she weakly gestured for her to bring her to the bed. Both friends took opposite sides of her and supported the baby in her embrace. There was a look of almost otherworldly love when she gazed down at her daughter, a silent tear tracking down her gaunt cheek. "Do you remember the last Christmas we all had together here on the ranch? Bennett swore he was going to cook everyone the perfect turkey."

"And then got distracted with the boys," Evelyn added.

"I still don't know how he managed to get the outside of that bird completely black and the inside absolutely raw." Misty shook her head in amazement at the dead man's talents.

"And then we all had mashed potatoes and green beans

with cranberry sauce." Indie gave a chuckle that ended in her struggling for air. Misty cast a worried glance at Evelyn, one that she could only answer with a helpless shrug.

"That was the best time of my life." She gently squeezed each of her friends' hands, her skin paper thin. "Thank you for being my friends all these years. It's okay, you have to let me go now. It's time. I'm so tired." Evelyn's eyes swam with tears as her friend gave her a serene smile. "Evelyn, you need to somehow make it okay with Colt, too. I've tried, but he's not ready to hear it yet." Indie placed a gentle kiss on her daughter's head. "Tell my baby I love her every single day and it was all worth it to be able to be her mama."

Evelyn gulped hard, hot tears streaming down her face. Across from her, Misty bravely fought to keep her despair at bay and failed. "I promise."

"Every step she takes, I'll be there watching over her with her daddy. Even if she can't see us, she needs to know we'll be there." Indie took a deep shuddering breath and held an arm out wide. "Come here." The girls hugged her as if they never wanted to let her go, knowing deep down that this would be the last time. "I love you guys."

"We love you, too."

"Will you stay with me?" Indie's voice was now a weak whisper as if her speech had sapped the last of her strength.

"You'd have to drag us away." Misty said, sniffling. "And even then, we'd fight to get back."

"Please just hold me and talk about when we were young." Indie's voice sounded far away, drifting off to sleep.

"Speak for yourself, I'm still young," denied Misty.

"I remember when you got your braces stuck on Logan's under the bleachers." A smile ghosted Indie's blue-tinged lips.

Evelyn hooted. "And Bennett and Colt getting some wire cutters to set you both free. Your mom was furious and said that you would have to pay the bill."

"I remember how handsome Bennett was when he took me to the prom." Indie wheezed.

"You wore that beautiful red dress." Evelyn remembered it like it was yesterday. "And we all shared a limo together."

"And Logan snuck some beers from his dad and spilled them over my dress." Misty glowered at the memory. "You went with the exchange student," she teased Evelyn.

"And then after the prom, we all went out to Rush Creek and the boys built a fire and we stayed there talking till the sun came up. You remember, Indie?"

"I remember everything." Her voice was now a thin thread over the rattle in her chest. "Promise to remember me."

Outside an owl hooted as Evelyn rested her forehead against Indie's, her tears splashing onto her friend's face. "How could I ever forget my best friend?" No answer was forthcoming except for the steady rattle of Indie breathing.

CHAPTER 11

*S*unlight caught the translucent colors inside the heart, twisting and swirling sunflower yellow into the scarlet red and royal blue. Evelyn marveled that she could still see anything that wasn't a shade of gray. If she hadn't had Hope to continue caring for, she would have gladly curled up into a ball and hidden from the world like a wounded animal.

The baby reached her chubby hand out to capture the glass heart. "Hope, my darling, do you see that yellow? That's your mama's color. I don't think there was ever a room she walked into that she didn't light up." Evelyn blinked furiously. *I am not going to start crying. Not today. Today, Colt needs me to be strong for him.*

Immaculate in a designer black dress, Misty stepped into the nursery, her red lipstick only serving to highlight her pale drawn features. "Colt's ready to leave. Are you and Hope ready?"

Ready to say goodbye to her best friend, one who had been closer to her than a sister, whose daughter she now cradled in her arms? How was she ever meant to be ready for that? Carefully placing the glass sculpture into the diaper bag, she headed for the door, a lump set like concrete in her chest making it feel like she would never breathe freely again. *For Indie. I can do this for her.*

~

THE PASTOR HAD SAID some words, probably about how great a person Indie was—*had been.* Colt wanted to scream at him that he didn't know the half of it. His kid sister. She was more than just some adjectives spoken into the wind. She'd been everything that had been good in his life and he'd failed her. He felt like the sun had gone away and he wasn't sure how he was going to survive in the dark.

Colt sat as people milled around him, only dimly aware of the drive back to the ranch—a place that now only served to remind him of his failure. He was vaguely aware of Logan and Shelby sitting with him on the porch, Trixie trying to get him to eat something before he was left to his grief. Colt's freshly starched collar rubbed abrasively against his neck, his boots pinching his feet. The chatter inside was quiet now, the last mourner having left hours ago, clutching thick wads of tissue in their hands. And yet, still, he sat.

It was the smell of her perfume that broke through the fog first. Evelyn had worn that same fragrance since she was thirteen. In a dark room, he would have been able to find her simply by following the trail of jasmine, lemons, fresh grass and sunshine. The swing rocked as she settled herself beside him, not saying a word as she simply stared out at the vista before them.

"What do I do, Evelyn?" Colt knew she would understand. She always had.

"Live, I guess." Her smile was bittersweet as she swung her legs. "I know that's what Indie wanted."

Colt's fury sliced through him. "What Indie wanted? Don't you think Indie would have wanted to live?" He didn't care if he hurt her or not.

"Of course she wanted to live. We all wanted her to. But at the end, she was ready. She had nothing left to fight with." Evelyn laid a comforting hand on his arm. Colt didn't want to see her pitying eyes. Angrily, he shrugged her off. The silence stretched between them, and Evelyn licked her lips, opening her mouth before snapping it shut again.

"I'm going back on the road."

Her deep blue eyes darkened like thunderclouds. "What about Hope?"

He snorted contemptuously. "Some hope she turned out to be. I don't care. I'll hire a nanny."

"But she needs you!" Evelyn glanced sharply at him, her lips compressed into a sharp line.

Anger and something else—something he didn't want to delve too deeply into—singed the corners of his soul at the accusing look. "My life is on the road doing rodeos. At least when I'm doing that, I know what my job is and I'm good at it. I have control."

"But Hope needs her family. You're all she has left." Evelyn's voice was cold and lashing.

The last remaining thread of Colt's restraint snapped, sending him spiraling dangerously. "I wish she never exist-ed." Bitterness contorted his face. "At least then I'd still have my sister."

Evelyn gasped in horror, her face paling. "You don't know that, and you definitely don't mean it. I'll stay on to take care of her. I know you're hurting right now. Maybe going on the road will give you the space you need to work through it all."

"I'm fine," he snarled. "I'm going on the road because that's where I want to be."

He pushed off the swing, setting it to rocking furiously, and strode away. A whisper on the breeze floated after him. "And I'm here because it's where I'm needed." Her soft words stung as scathingly as if she'd screamed them at him, and he fled into the sepia-toned evening.

CHAPTER 12

*H*ope began to fuss on Evelyn's hip as she balanced her phone against her ear and signed for the gold sports car that had just been unloaded. It was the third one that had been delivered that month. She smiled as she handed the clipboard back to the man, returning to her conversation.

"Yes, I understand that it is a great honor to be asked to make the sculpture. But as it's a significant piece, I'm not sure I currently have the capacity to produce it, let alone within the time constraints the client has requested."

Her agent breathed down the line in annoyance. "Evelyn, you've been on hiatus long enough. I don't want you to throw away your career as you slowly grow moldy in the country." Crisp British tones gave an insulting edge to the observation. "I'll go back to the client and see if I can get them to budge on the deadline, but if I do, my dear, I expect you to take this commission. You are a working artist after all, not a retired one."

"I don't know. Maybe if I retire, my current work will become more exclusive and get you higher prices."

"Don't tempt me. And we still need to agree on dates for your exhibition."

Hope began to wail, her chubby face turning beet red under the onslaught of her emotions. "I need to go. Email me dates, and I'll look them over." Evelyn wrinkled her nose at the pungent aroma wafting from the baby's diaper.

"I emailed them to you last month and you said you'd look over them then." Icy disapproval fairly froze the connection.

Evelyn bit back a sigh, wincing as Hope took her screaming up a notch. Somewhere there was bound to be a pack of dogs howling back. "It's been hectic, but this time I promise I'll look at it." She quickly hung up before she could hear another word from her agent and blew out her cheeks. "Come on, Miss Stinkypants, we'd better get you changed."

As she changed the loaded diaper, she found herself staring at the gold Italian sportscar in the drive. Her nerves began to tingle with resentment that Colt was off having a playboy billionaire bachelor lifestyle. The last she'd heard was that he'd decided to try his hand at NASCAR racing, and to that end, had purchased a team. It had to be true since she'd seen the social media photos of him drinking champagne from giant bottles surrounded by a bevy of scantily clad women. There he was with no responsibilities, and she was left holding the baby. Heck, she hadn't even figured out how to be a mom and keep her career, which her agent seemed to delight in reminding her.

Evelyn glanced at her watch. Misty should have arrived by now. Before she could even finish the thought, the staccato of helicopter blades thundered against her chest, the front yard filling with swirling dust and debris. *Now I know how Dorothy felt.* Apparently her friend was traveling from the airport in style.

Evelyn glanced around the nursery, taking it all in. The

dusky pink wallpaper with framed delicate watercolors that Indie had just had to have, bidding eye-watering amounts on Colt's credit card. The cashmere carpet she'd insisted on because no daughter of hers was going to get carpet burn learning to crawl. Evelyn smiled. Indie had always been down to earth, but she sure had burned through a lot of her brother's cash for her daughter. She closed her eyes as she ran her hand over the edge of the cradle.

In her mind's eye, Indie was healthy and happy, rocking her baby gently by the flickering fireplace as she crooned lullabies. Opening them again, she came crashing back to reality. Shaking at the tremendous responsibility that she felt ill equipped to undertake, she struggled to breathe as her fears choked her. She didn't have time for this. She needed to be strong no matter how much it felt like she was falling about at the seams. Indie was relying on her to be here for her daughter. Slowly the vicelike grip on her heart loosened and she was simply standing in a nursery holding a baby.

"Hey, I thought I'd find you in here." Misty scrunched her face up in protest, frantically waving her hand in front of her and gasping for air. "By all that is holy, that is one powerful smell."

"This little cherub's superpowers are being cute and adept at clearing a room with a single dirty diaper." Evelyn hugged her friend with her free arm, thankful that she hadn't noticed her distress, before handing the miniature superhero over. "Good flight?"

"Yeah, and did you see my new toy?" Misty looked like a kid on Christmas morning.

"That little thing that just landed in my front yard and got Colt's new toy all dirty in the process?"

Misty quirked a brow at her. "Your front yard? I thought it was Colt's. Unless there's something you want to tell me?"

Evelyn could feel herself growing warm under her

friend's teasing glance. Why had that slipped out? Sure, she'd spent more time there lately than Colt, but she'd sounded downright possessive. "You know what I mean."

"Sure I do. Colt and Evelyn sitting in a tree, k-i-s-s-i-n-g."

"He'd have to be here for any kissing." *Why the heck is my brain letting my mouth run like that?*

"So, what you are saying is that if he showed up right now, you'd finally make a move on him." To drive her point home, Misty proceeded to make kissy faces. Evelyn threw a pillow at her. "Hey, remember the dear child."

"Did I hit her?' Evelyn circled, ready to dodge the return shot.

"No, but that was down to sheer luck." Hope began to wave her fists in the air. "You poor child. Auntie Evelyn is so mean. It's a good think Auntie Misty is here to protect you."

"Mean?" Evelyn snorted. "She knows she has me wrapped around her little finger."

"Which is a good thing. When was the last time Colt came home, or intends to for that matter?" Evelyn hated the way Misty looked at her, her mouth set in a disapproving line. "William mentioned he's made an offer on the Dallas Cowboys. He's too young to be having a mid-life crisis."

"He's just dealing with things in his own way." *I wish he'd let me help him, but apparently he doesn't want anything to do with me right now.*

Keen eyes took her unspoken words. "If it's all getting too hard being here, especially with how you feel about Colt, why don't you just leave? Take Hope and head home. Or heck, I'd love to have the both of you move in with me in New York."

Evelyn snorted. "Your penthouse is the most un-kid-friendly environment I could possibly think of to expose Hope to."

Misty shrugged. "How about my Hampton's place? Now

that I have the helicopter, I can fly up on the weekends. Heck, Hope would love it when I visit Chora and the animals at her shelter."

"No, Colt needs me here." In her heart, she believed it with every fiber of her being.

"He sure has a funny way of showing it. I mean, I miss Indie too."

"He's grieving—we all are. And you're wrong. He does need me. People either do two things with love. They're either showing it or they're crying out for it. I'm showing it and Colt, well"—she looked at Misty, her passionate belief strumming through her blood—"he's crying out for it, he just hasn't figured it out yet. He's like a wounded animal. Existing just to react, chasing the next thrill that will make him forget the pain for a while." Evelyn's determination was like a rock inside of her.

Misty gently placed her free hand on Evelyn's forearm. "You're the only best friend I have left, and you know I love Colt like a brother, but if he hurts you..." Her expression turned icy. "He won't like what I have to say about it—or do it about it, for that matter. But he better wake up to himself soon. The Evelyn I know is too good to spend her life waiting for a man." Misty's gaze drilled into her, a probing query in her eyes.

Evelyn was the first to break contact, biting her lip. Wasn't that what she'd spent her entire life doing? Waiting for him to notice her?

~

HIS DRINKING COMPANIONS giggled as the world spun on its axis around Colt, blurring it until it was nothing but a mess of shapeless colors and sounds. The bottle in his hand remained the only thing real, solid in his hands as he brought it to his lips. He couldn't even remember what they were celebrating—or if they were, in fact, celebrating at all. All he knew was the comforting numbness that spread through him, releasing him from thoughts of dark-eyed angels waiting for him at home or the baby who kept him away.

Colt shuddered, the intrusive thoughts killing his buzz. He was, however, now an expert on how to remedy the situation. "Who wants to see how fast my new car can go?"

Staggering to his feet, bottle clutched tightly, he made his way over, a vapid blonde under each arm. With another guzzle from the bottle, liquid splashing down his chin, he slumped into the driver's seat, his head lolling forward as blackness claimed him.

THE LONG DRIVE looked the same, graveled and lined with pristine white post-and-rail fences, the house waiting at the end. Colt gripped the steering wheel tightly with damp hands, perspiration clammy on his forehead as he fought the darkness that gibbered at him. Nausea churned in his stomach, sour bile stinging the back of his throat. He flung the door of his truck open and vomited.

Spent, he took a slug from his water bottle, gulping it down before swishing it around his mouth and spitting it out onto the ground. Wiping the moisture away with the back of his hand, he pulled the door closed. When he was away, he could pretend Indie and Bennett were a phone call away. But now ... now he would have to deal with the stark reality that Indie wasn't there waiting for him.

Knocking his truck into gear, he grimly drove on, ignoring the whispered suggestions of his fevered mind to turn it around and get the heck out of there and go anywhere that wasn't here. Colt wasn't sure how he got to the end of the drive or how long he sat in his car when he did. Blinking, he looked around, surprised to see Evelyn walking down the steps of the porch, Hope in her arms. Hatred snaked inside him, biting into his soul at the sight of her holding the baby who'd killed his sister.

Thrusting the door open, he brushed passed her, ignoring the startled exclamation at his rudeness to her homecoming welcome and unlatched the tailgate of the trailer. He could hear Big Wheels impatiently pawing to be let out. It seemed like the chestnut was at least happy to be home. Without casting another look in their direction, he stalked to the barn.

His horse's customary stall was laid with fresh straw, the water bucket sparkling clean. Colt unclipped the lead and left Big Wheels to settle in as he grabbed a pail of feed and filled the manger. Once he was satisfied his mount was taken care of, he went in search of his prey. Moving several crates aside, his searching fingers grasped the smooth, cool glass. *Come to Daddy.*

Colt pulled the bottle of whiskey out from its place of confinement and sat down on one of the upturned crates. Taking a slug, he looked around in satisfaction. The new farmhand he'd put on to help around the ranch seemed to be more than up to the task. He made a mental note to give him a bonus, and heck, he could have a pay increase too. Another mouthful of the amber liquid slid smoothly down his throat, the burning leaving the beginning of pleasant numbness behind in its wake. A few more, and somehow being back at the ranch didn't feel so bad.

"Colt Justice Montgomery." Evelyn flew through the doorway and into the aisle of the barn, blue eyes wide as she scanned the building trying to locate him, her hands firmly planted on those curvy hips of hers. Colt couldn't remember the last time she looked so sexy—and there'd be plenty over the years.

"Yes, gorgeous?" The words felt thick on his tongue. Experimentally, he ran it over his teeth.

Her dark hair swirled as she rounded on him, following the sound of his voice, the cleft in her chin thrust out as she glared at him. *Damn, but she was adorable.* "You have a lot of explaining to do, mister." She marched over and stabbed him in the chest with her finger. "And you better start now."

"What would you like to hear?" Colt gave her his best heavy-lidded smirk, the one that never failed to get the ladies all hot and bothered.

Evelyn blinked at him, as if unsure how to proceed. Furrowing her brows at him, she recaptured her momentum. "Colt, I've made lots of excuses for you to Misty—heck, to myself—but I will not tolerate being treated like a doormat and ignored when you finally decide to grace us with your presence." She appeared to spy the bottle in his hand for the first time. "Are you drinking?"

"I'm a grown-arse man and I'll do what I darn well want." Colt spat the words at her.

"Well, start acting like one then," she blazed right back at him.

"It doesn't matter."

Evelyn took pause, cocking her head at him like some exotic bird staring down a worm—or worse, a slug. "What doesn't matter? How you're acting?"

"All of this," Colt's arm flailed about, attempting to gesture around. "The toys, my money, this ranch. I'm a goddamn billionaire, and what good did it do? It didn't save Indie. I couldn't save my baby sister." Raw grief ripped at his insides, the darkness beckoning to him. "And now I'm all alone."

"Enough with the pity party." Evelyn's voice slashed at him like a whip. He jerked at the stinging rebuttal. "You don't think I lost anything? I lost her too, you know. She was my best friend, but she was so much more than that. I can't even begin to imagine all the things that I want to share with her, talk about, have a wine and giggle about some silly little thing that happened." Evelyn's head was majestically thrown back as she drew in a deep, shuddering breath. "But she isn't here, and I can't change that no matter how much I wish and pray." Her voice shook as she spoke, and anguish blazed at him from her eyes. "And believe me, I've done plenty of both since you ran away and left me here alone."

Colt guiltily looked away, taking another long drink of whiskey, realizing for the first time that he wasn't the only one struggling, that Evelyn had been struggling—and with the baby, too. But Evelyn wouldn't allow him to escape that easily. She moved until he was forced to look at her.

"But her baby is still here." Her voice softened with love. "This is the last piece I have left of her—one that I can kiss, and tickle her little feet. And sometimes it feels like Indie is still here, watching over my shoulder, especially when I tell Hope how much her mama loved her." Evelyn's voice broke, crystalline tears cascading down her face. "You know I tell her stories about Indie all the time, and it hurts, but sometimes I smile through the tears. Pretending Hope doesn't exist isn't healthy for anyone. Not her, not you, not me." Exhausted from the passionate speech, she collapsed on the empty crate beside him and, grabbing the bottle from his hands, took a long drink.

Despair washed away the numbness, and drunkenly, he began to sob. Evelyn gathered him in her arms, tenderly brushing the hair away from his forehead as she rocked back and forth as if he were a child whose wound she could make better with a simple kiss. Outside in the deepening twilight, crickets began to chirp. As Colt listened to their background to Evelyn's crooning, he wished it was so simple.

CHAPTER 13

*I*t was his eyes that made her feel like crying. Bloodshot and filled with torment. It was like a window into Colt's soul, brittle and empty. Last night, Evelyn had stayed with him until his grief had run its course, and then made sure he got to bed. But this morning she could see the same demons riding his shoulders. She loved this broken man sitting hunched in his chair across the large kitchen table from her, and it killed her to see him like this and not be able to magically make things better. *Unfortunately, this is something Colt's going to have to figure out for himself.*

Setting the baby monitor on the table, she leaned forward, wrapping both hands as if for support around her gold-rimmed coffee mug. "I accepted the biggest commission of my career yesterday."

"You deserve it. You're one heck of an artist." Colt squinted at her, as if even the dim light caused him untold pain.

"Thank you. And I've finally given a date to my agent for an exhibition in London." Evelyn paused to take another sip of her coffee, stalling, unsure how he would take what she was going to say next. "But I need to get back to my real studio to do it all. The place I rented here isn't really set up for the scale I need."

Colt gave a sharp nod, his broad chest rising as he drew in a deep breath. "I think now is the best time to discuss the baby."

"Her name is Hope," Evelyn replied sharply, unease prickling up her spine. He couldn't even say her name. Whatever he was going to say next was not going to be pleasant.

"I think the best thing for *Hope*"—he stressed the word, his mouth puckering in distaste as though even saying it left a sour taste in his mouth—"would be for her to be adopted by a family who wants her." Evelyn's mouth fell open in stunned horror. Not noticing—or perhaps uncaring—Colt continued twisting the knife. "Obviously, the Gray's would love to have her, but given their health situations and age, they're not in a position to take on the responsibility."

"You've already spoken to them?" She spoke in a suffocated whisper. *They hadn't even been out to visit her once since she was born. How dare he contact them behind her back!*

"Yes, several days ago."

Evelyn wasn't even sure if she knew the man sitting across from her, his gaze sliding past her into the distance. Fury choked her, bottling up her emotions until, like a soda can that had been given one shake too many, she exploded. "How. Dare. You."

"Evelyn, I—"

"No, you don't get to speak right now. Not after saying that to me." Evelyn's voice hardened ruthlessly. Colt looked down, tracing circles of moisture left by his cup on the table. "You come back here after being away for months and tell me that you've decided to give Hope away. YOU!" Venom ripped from her throat. "Obviously, I wasted my breath last night. You didn't listen to a single damn thing I said. You'd already made up your mind."

"I did listen. Evelyn—" Those green eyes that had always made her knees melt pleaded with her. "It's why I'm doing this. I don't know if I'll ever be able to forgive that baby for making me lose Indie. But regardless, it's not fair to her to be in a household and have that projected on her. And you just said yourself that you need to get back to your career. Another family would be a better option for her. One that will love her."

"Love her?" Pained disbelief shredded her vocal cords. "She is cherished, she is loved, and you know who by? ME!" Evelyn could barely see Colt through her tears as she screamed her betrayal at him. "She isn't going anywhere. This little girl is now as much a part of me as she was of Indie, and I will never let her go. Indie would be ashamed of you—as disgusted as I am to even look at you—that you would throw Hope away like a piece of garbage." Evelyn stared at him in contempt, his familiar features now belonging to a stranger.

"I can't do it, don't you understand? When I look at her, all I see is what killed my baby sister. She's the reason Indie isn't here anymore." Colt bellowed his pain at her, spit flying from his mouth.

Evelyn's throat thickened, shards of ice piercing her heart. She raised her chin and stared at him defiantly, blinking away her tears. "That's where we're different. I see a piece of my best friend when I look at Hope, and if you'd let her"—*and me*—"your savior, too." Knowing that if she stayed there any longer what remained of her heart would shatter, she dashed from the room.

≈

ONE OF THE benefits of having a mansion was if one chose to avoid someone, it was entirely possible to do so for weeks. At this point, Colt wasn't entirely sure if he was the avoider or the avoidee. Heck, he was probably both. He'd manage to rise early, often already tending to his stock before Chase, his ranch hand, arrived. And Big Wheels had never looked so fit in his life. Working the cattle had honed the big chestnut into peak physical condition. It seemed a pity that it wasn't going to be seen in the arena anytime soon.

It was easy to fill his days with a myriad of things that left him exhausted by bedtime and not needing to delve too deeply into the festering wound of his soul. A ranch was a good place to lose yourself—as long as he could stop himself from staring up at the house, thinking about the woman and baby inside.

It was only as he lay in his bed on his silky satin sheets, surrounded by his trophy buckles, that loneliness tugged at him. Indie had been his family, but somehow, over the years, it was Evelyn who had provided him with a shoulder to lean on, the one who could share a gaze with him across a crowded room, somehow making him feel better just knowing she was there. Sure, Logan and Bennett had been his best friends, but in her own way, so was Evelyn. Maybe more so.

Now she couldn't stand to be in the same room as him, and if she hated him, it wasn't half as much as he despised himself. But whenever he thought of that baby, pain tormented him, anguish dancing through his soul. Once she was gone, he didn't need to ever think about her again, and maybe he might be free of this agony that cankered his heart.

It turned out, as he stared down at the paperwork his lawyer had drawn up for any potential parents for Hope, that it was just another brick to weigh him down, forcing him under until he couldn't breathe from the guilt. Staggering under his burden, he headed to the barn where he knew he could find respite in the company of a bottle and his horse.

"You know, Big Wheels, you and me, we're just regular cowboys ... well, maybe a cow-horse for you." Whiskey slushed from the bottle as he waved it about. Owlishly, he blinked at where it had spilled on his shirt. What a waste of fine aged liquor. "I mean, how many buckles do we need? We know we're the best."

"So was your father." Evelyn's soft voice sounded tired. *No, that wasn't right. She sounds defeated.*

"I'll drink to that." He raised his bottle in salute to her before gulping the numbing elixir down. "Heck, I think Dad deserves two."

Evelyn's periwinkle blue eyes no longer sparkled, they just looked sad. Colt wondered when he'd last seen them shimmer at him, the corners of her mouth tilting up as they shared a private joke between them. Now that he thought about it, he couldn't remember the last time he'd felt happy either, or even just normal.

"I came to tell you that I've started making arrangements to leave. I should have them finalized any day now." Colt shriveled at her words, ice spreading through his stomach. He downed another shot, waiting for the numbness to follow.

"You don't have to go."

"Yes, I do." Tears bordered her eyes as she tried to blink them away. Her bottom lip trembled and, losing the fight, they cascaded down her cheeks.

Colt found himself standing in front of her. His hands slipped up her arms, bringing her closer. He could feel her uneven breathing on his cheek as he held her. He found that he had no desire to step out of this embrace. It was like he'd found himself in a waking dream. Without thought and marveling at how right it felt, he tenderly tilted her chin up so he could stare into her glorious eyes, the lashes now damp spikes. Knowing he couldn't walk away now if he tried, he slowly lowered his mouth to hers in a kiss that was as tender and light as a summer breeze. The touch of her lips on his sent shockwaves through his entire body.

And the slap of her hand on his cheek reverberated through his skull. *This wasn't how it was meant to end.* At least not in any dream he'd ever had about Evelyn. The thought forced its way through his drunken stupor.

"I'm not some cheap floozie you can use to make yourself feel better. I deserve more respect than that, Colt Montgomery." She glared at him with burning reproachful eyes.

"Evelyn, I didn't mean anything by it." *Darn, he hated that he'd hurt her. Everything was such a mess.*

"You never do, Colt. I wasn't sure before, but now I know that it really is for the best that Hope and I are leaving."

Soul-destroying guilt lashed at him. He'd driven her away —the last person he'd ever wanted to do that to. "Evelyn, I'm sorry."

"Yeah, well, me too."

Colt floundered in an agonizing maelstrom, terrible regrets assailing him. "I know she's just a baby, and I hate myself that I can't love her." At the sound of his voice, she lifted her head and looked at him like he was the lowest of the low.

"Just stop. I don't want to hear what you have to say, or be around you anymore. What you've become is so ugly. But before I go and never come back, I want to tell you something. Not for you, but for me, so I can move on. I've spent my entire life loving you from afar." She shook her head sadly. "I don't think you'll ever fully appreciate just how much I desperately wanted to be the one to put all your broken pieces back together. But now I realize that all it would do is end in madness for me."

"Evelyn—" He reached out for her, but she moved away, his hand falling uselessly to his side.

"I prayed that Hope would help you become the man you were supposed to be, the man she needs you to be. But only you can want that for you, not me. I really hope you're hearing what I'm saying somewhere in that drink-addled brain of yours, because this is my last attempt to get you to see—and I mean really see—what you have in front of you if you're just brave enough to accept it. But I can't keep being around, watching you destroy yourself, hating everything and everyone around you. But most especially yourself. I don't want to feel like I've wasted all those years loving you, idolizing you. So, I'm going to leave while I still have memories that aren't tarnished." Evelyn gave him a sad little smile. "Goodbye, Colt."

A raw primitive grief overwhelmed him. His anguish peaked to shatter the last shreds of control. "Evelyn!"

But this time, for the first time ever in their lives, she didn't come when he needed her. A sensation of intense sickness and desolation swept over him as she disappeared from view. Colt covered his face with trembling hands and gave vent to the agony of his loss.

CHAPTER 14

*H*ow was it possible that the light sneaking through the cracks in Colt's eyelids should pierce into his brain with the force of sledgehammers? Or that his tongue should be stuck to the roof of his dry mouth with the ferocity of gum to the bottom of a shoe? And yet, here he was, yet again. *I'm getting too old for this.* He knew deep inside that after last night, the day of reckoning had arrived.

Colt grimaced, imagining what Indie would have had to say, knowing it would have been bad. Heck, the worst bit was that he'd finally kissed Evelyn after all those years of waiting and it had turned out to be an epic drunken disaster. The thought barely registered before another followed. He thought about his sister, and agony twisted at his insides, clawing at his sanity.

Colt's eyes sprung open at the realization, only for him to groan at the sudden movement. *Maybe Indie was punishing him for his bad behavior from beyond.* He smiled. He liked the idea of her still being around, watching over him like some sort of bossy angel.

"I'm going to do better, Indie. I promise," he whispered, gingerly swinging his legs over the edge of the bed, a wave a nausea rushing up to greet him. "Yeah, I deserved that." Stumbling to the shower, he rubbed at the stubble on his chin. *Time for a shave, too.* Then he had some things to set right.

Feeling like a million dollars—*make that a billion dollars*—after freshening up, he stepped into the kitchen, the high gloss counters and cabinetry reflecting laser beams of sunshine into his eyes. Wincing, he was nonetheless famished and ready to destroy whatever Trixie was willing to make. "Morning, Trixie."

The housekeeper pursed her lips and gave a disapproving sniff before turning back to pack the dishwasher.

Okay... "Did you sleep well last night?" Colt could charm the birds from the sky when he tried. At least, he used to be able to.

"I slept fine, thank you." Trixie's back was ramrod straight, fairly bristling with indignation.

"Any chance of one of your delicious breakfasts?" He gave her his best little boy look which was completely wasted since she refused to turn around. "I sure could use it this morning."

Trixie closed the dishwasher with enough force to startle several mockingbirds in the large tree outside the window. "Yes, boss. Whatever Colt wants, he gets."

He narrowed his eyes at her. "Is there something you want to say?"

"I would, if I thought for one second you would listen to anyone else but your own self-pity. If you won't listen to one of your best friends, I highly doubt you'll listen to a mere housekeeper." Finally, Trixie turned, skewering him with a look he hadn't seen since his mother had been alive. Well, he'd managed to make his housekeeper well and truly annoyed.

"Go for it. I deserve whatever it is you have to say."

She raised her brows so high he was amazed they didn't hit the exposed timber beams in the ceiling. He winced. *Yep, I'm in for it now.*

"It was my privilege to have known Indie, if only for a little time, but I'd like to think that I knew her. From what I saw, there was only one thing she cared about and that was family. You"—Trixie jabbed a finger at him, making Colt thankful he wasn't closer—"Misty, Evelyn and that baby. And from what I've seen, as soon as she died, you've done your darndest to drive everything she loved away."

Colt was overwhelmed with the torment that had dogged every step he'd taken since Indie died. Darn, he'd made so many mistakes and hurt everyone who'd tried to help him, but mostly Evelyn and Hope. Heck, he could spend the rest of his life trying to make it right and still not come close. He looked down at the floor, unwilling to see the condemnation in the older woman's eyes.

"I'm gonna make it right, I swear. Heck, I have all these plans."

Trixie gave a tight nod, obviously not willing to trust him yet. *I don't blame her.* "You better hurry."

"What do you mean?" His heartrate accelerated alarmingly, beads of perspiration gathering on his brow.

"Evelyn is packing her things. She was meant to leave at the end of the month, but this morning she said she couldn't bear to spend a minute longer on this ranch."

Colt only half listened to the housekeeper as he struggled with his conscience. He was the reason Evelyn couldn't stay. Last night had been the final straw for her, and he couldn't fault her for it. A certainty took grip. He would not lose her too—not now, not when he was finally seeing glimpses of color amongst the gray. Whatever it took, he was going to do it. Evelyn was worth it, even if it meant that he needed to finally face Hope and what she represented.

~

HOPE LAY on the blanket Evelyn had spread out for her in the middle of the nursery, watching with wide eyes as she rolled from side to side. *Any minute now.* Evelyn sat on the edge of her seat, anticipation building, certain today was the day she would crawl over to her. She heaved a sigh. Watching the baby wasn't going to make this go any faster. Internally, she debated what she could, in good conscience, take with her. After all, Colt had made it crystal clear that he wanted nothing to do with Hope, so why would he need a fully furnished nursery?

The mere thought of him was enough to break the wall of her self-control. How dare he get drunk and kiss her last night! She didn't know if she was angrier at him for kissing her or herself for allowing him to. In that moment when his lips had brushed hers, she'd felt a dizzying current race through her. And in that instant, she'd pretended that he'd kissed her because he cared about her—had feelings for her —not as a drunken distraction from his pain.

Evelyn sunk to the plush carpet, tears blurring her vision into a swirl of cream and pink. Hope gave a little giggle and army crawled across the floor to her, headbutting Evelyn's leg before using it to pull herself up on. Evelyn picked her up and laid her back on the floor to blow raspberries on her squishy belly. Delighted giggles soothed the sharp edges of her hurt. Colt was the past, Hope was the future. But darn if it didn't hurt so bad.

Evelyn's head jerked up at the soft, almost tentative

knock at the door, her insides quivering at the sight of Colt, hat in hand, watching her intently. "May I come in?"

"It's your house, I can't stop you." Bitterness laced each and every word. It felt like she was leaving home—one that had filled such a cherished place in her heart for so long.

"Evelyn, this house will always be here for you."

Rage blinded her at his words. "Really?" Sarcasm dripped from each syllable. "Somehow I don't think I'll be coming back once I'm gone." She hated how much that pained her to think about. "I think it's only fair to tell you that I'm taking all of Hope's things with me. I think it's the least you can do for your niece." Evelyn's throat felt raw with unuttered screams and protests. She wanted to beat on his chest, to claw at his face and make him hurt the way she was hurting. *But I guess he already is. Just not for me or Hope.*

Remorse and anguish lay naked in his gaze. "You can take whatever you want, but can you come with me first? Please?" Colt shoved his hands in his pockets, hunching his shoulders.

Evelyn's anger blew out like a candle in a breeze. Defeated, she acknowledged silently to herself that no one was emerging from this sad situation as a winner. They were all losing something. Someone. "Fine, Colt, but then I need to get straight back to packing."

She bent down to scoop up a dribbling Hope and placed her on her hip. The poor thing was teething again, but she had such a sunny disposition she didn't grizzle despite her discomfort. In what would have once been companionable silence, now was awkward and tense between them as they made their way through the hallways of the large house. *I wonder where he's taking me.* A prickle of anticipation danced up her spine, setting her nerves to tingling and washing away her apathy in its wake. *Why the mystery?*

A cacophony of noise enveloped her as she stepped out onto the porch, her mouth falling open in surprise. Work trucks and men milled around, some unpacking lumber, others tools.

"What's going on?" Bafflement made her voice sharp.

Colt surveyed the controlled chaos in front of him with an air of satisfaction tempered with uncertainty. He turned, his eyes catching and holding hers. "They're building you a studio."

"But why? I'm leaving," she stammered in bewilderment. Her treacherous heart flooded with hope, and not just the kind waving pudgy hands at the workers.

"I know I've done so many things wrong by both you and Hope. I never meant to make you feel like our friendship didn't mean anything to me. It does. It's actually one of the few things in my life that is priceless, and it's time I start acting like it." He swallowed, looking in the distance as though gathering his thoughts, and cleared his throat. "I don't know much about babies. Heck, I'm not even sure I'm the kind of man Hope needs in her life. I can't promise tomorrow that I'm going to wake up loving her, but I'll try. Maybe start with not hating her for something that wasn't her fault."

All of her loneliness and confusion welded together in an upsurge of devouring yearning. "I don't know." Regret underlined her confusion. "There's been a lot of damage done."

Colt reached out, his fingers warm and strong where they touched hers. "I know, and I don't blame you for not trusting me when I say it won't happen again. I got in touch with Misty. She sent through some recommendations for therapists. Not just for me to work through my baggage, but also a family therapist for all of us. To be the best family we can be." His compelling green eyes had a sheen of purpose. Evelyn found herself being drawn in, despite herself. "I guess what I'm asking is if you and Hope will stay."

"And you're building me a studio so I can work?"

"I'm building you a studio so you can work," he agreed, hope flickering to life in his eyes.

"And you're going to start therapy?"

"Yes, ma'am, with the best in the country."

Evelyn bit down on her bottom lip, uncertain how much she was willing to risk being hurt again. How much she could risk Hope being hurt as well. "Colt, you've hurt us a lot, and I'm not sure how easy it's going to be to mend those fences, but I know Indie would want me to try." She said the words tentatively, as if testing the idea. "So, we'll try. For now."

He gave her a smile that set her bruised heart racing. "I won't ever make the same mistakes again. I've been living like there was nothing but darkness, and now that I feel the light shining on me again, I'm never going back to that place."

Evelyn prayed that he meant it for all their sakes.

CHAPTER 15

"And do you see over there, Hope?" Colt gestured to the construction in front of them as Evelyn held the babe snugly on her hip. For a little thing, she sure had a lot of energy. *Just like Indie.* He smiled as he squinted into the sun, pointing out where the builders were up on the roof of the new studio. "Those men are putting the roofing on, and then Evelyn will be all set to start unpacking her things." Colt brought his face in close. "Do you think she'll like it?" he asked in a dramatically staged whisper. Hope kicked her legs about, giving delicious little girl giggles as she batted her lashes at him. *The kid was a first-class charmer.* It wasn't really surprising. He was her uncle, after all.

"I think I'm a lucky gal."

Colt wondered if Evelyn knew just how captivating she looked standing there with a baby on her hip as she was lit by the sun, her blue eyes sparkling as she grinned over at him. Probably not, but it sure as heck made him feel like a billion dollars—and he should know.

He looked back at the woman holding his niece. "I'm the

lucky one." Hope planted a sloppy kiss on his cheek, the cracks in the ice around his heart now in full thaw. "Well, if you're going to be like that."

He gently tickled her belly, enjoying the screeches of childish laughter that erupted from her. His therapist had warned him that it was going to take baby steps to heal the wounds of the past. Somehow, once he'd reached dead bottom and glimpsed what he really had to lose, he'd managed to shed some of the anger. Sure, he didn't feel comfortable settling her to sleep yet or giving her a bath, but in moments like this, he could allow himself to feel contentment in the baby's company. For now, that was enough.

"It's going to be great once I have everything I need here. But on that note, I need to head back inside and start working on my sketches." The breeze gently wafted Evelyn's dark hair around her heart-shaped face as she spoke, eyes thoughtful like she'd already begun picturing ideas. "Trixie said she can watch over Hope."

"The munchkin can stay with me for a while. I don't really have anything urgent I need to do."

Evelyn nodded dubiously. "Yeah, sure, I guess. If that's okay with you."

"Your lack of faith is hurtful." He gave Hope another tickle, setting her to giggling again. "We'll be fine. And if we get into trouble, I promise I'll find Trixie straightaway." He held up his palm. "Scout's honor." Hope grabbed at his hand, slightly ruining the solemn gesture.

"Well, I know when I've been beat. Colt, if you're going to spend more time out here in the sun, can you please make sure you put a hat on her?" Evelyn looked like she wanted to give more instructions but managed to restrain herself and handed the child over. Colt awkwardly juggled her about like his arms didn't know what to do as he gripped Hope. "Have fun, you two." With swaying hips, Evelyn left him alone with his niece. Colt was terrified. He just prayed that children weren't like livestock and couldn't smell his fear.

"Okay, kiddo, I think we've both spent enough time out here. How about we go find some toys to play with?" Since Hope didn't make an outright protest, Colt took that as a sign of agreeance. "And I know where there's a stash of them." With long, bouncy steps he headed back to the house.

Hope sneezed as he blew the dust off the top of the box. "Sorry."

He'd found an old blanket to sit her on, attempting to keep her off the dusty floorboards of the attic, but somehow, she'd managed to get cobwebs in her hair and a smudge on her face. *Better make sure she gets cleaned up before Evelyn sees her, otherwise we'll both be in trouble.* A smile tugged on his lips as he pictured the telling off he'd get. Evelyn was cute as heck when she was mad. He was willing to wager that she'd be none too happy to know that Hope was in the stale, dank air, but as soon as he found what he was after...

Opening the box, he began to fossick around inside. "Ahh!" he said in triumph. "Here we are." Colt looked at Hope to see her reaction, only to discover she'd found an old wooden skittle and was busy gnawing on the end of it. He quickly separated her from the germ carrier. "Yucky. What are you, part beaver?"

Hope just grinned at him, albeit with a dirty mouth. Guiltily, he scooped her up, his treasure in the other hand, and made for the door. "This is our secret. No telling on me." She pulled a face at him that he chose to believe was a pledge of secrecy. It did make it easier when your coconspirator couldn't talk yet. Jauntily, he headed for the nursery, feeling secure that they'd gotten away with their adventure.

❧

"Now, this is Chuck Bear, and he's the bestest teddy bear in the whole wide world." Colt's voice sounded slightly muffled as it drifted from the nursery. Evelyn paused on the verge of entering. For the first time it felt like she was intruding on a personal moment between them. "He went everywhere with me when I was a kid. Your grandpa was a famous bull rider, and when I was little, I used to travel around the rodeos with them. Your grandpa and grandma loved each other very much and sometimes it felt a little lonely. So, one day, they got Chuck Bear for me." Judging from the noise, something was being hit against the floor. Maybe a teapot? "A few years after that, your mama came along, and I was never lonely again."

Evelyn strained forward, the silence from Colt stretching. She wavered, almost about to enter, when he began to speak again. "Your mama used to take Chuck Bear all the time and make him all soggy. I'd get so mad at her." His voice thickened. "What I'd give to get mad at her one more time." More silence, broken by baby noises. "You sure are fast at crawling. Now, how about a cup of tea?"

Relief washed over Evelyn. She marveled at the progress she could hear in Colt's voice, admiring his vulnerability. Quietly turning, she tiptoed back down the hall, leaving the two alone to their tea party.

As the chattering nonsense and giggles fell away, a sense of loss infiltrated her spirit, urging her to turn around. *No,* she chided herself, *they're family and they need time to bond.* Setting her mouth in determination, she turned the lights of the conference room on, the bright whiteness making the edges of the polished timber gleam. With a sigh, she extracted her sketchpad from where she'd placed it neatly on the side cabinet and took a seat.

Staring at the rambling concepts she'd deftly drawn with

a few slick lines, she couldn't help but feel they were lacking. *Where's the passion? The feeling? That's why people buy an Evelyn Hart piece.* Her thoughts drifted back to the nursery, to the soulful green eyes that were once again filled with a joyful exuberance, shadows only tinging their depths from time to time. Evelyn's heart sung whenever he directed that gaze at her, but maybe she was misreading everything. Certainly, after the drunken kiss, all she'd felt was confused and saddened.

She jumped at the ring of her phone, muttering darkly under her breath at the harsh black pencil line that now dominated her page before skewing off the paper. "Hey, Misty."

"Hey, yourself. I'm checking in with how my favorite people are doing?"

"We're doing good. I'm working on some ideas for a commission."

"In the conference room?"

"Yes, why?" Evelyn bit back a smile as the big screen on the wall flickered to life, a request to join a meeting flashing urgently. Shaking her head, she reached into the center of the table to retrieve the controller and accept. "What makes you think I want to look at your face three feet high?"

"Well, I know you appreciate art, so I'm kinda like living art at those dimensions." Misty shook her long locks dramatically, letting them spill over her shoulders, and did her best supermodel pout.

"I'll take any inspiration at this point." Evelyn turned the ruined page over, tapping her pencil on the blank, stark whiteness. Giving up, she sighed. "Are you coming down this weekend?" She glanced hopefully at her friend's enormous face. Maybe what she needed was some girl time. They could get Trixie to watch Hope and have a few glasses of wine while watching some tragically bad eighties movie.

"Sorry, I need to catch up with Chora and go over a few things for next year's fundraising schedule."

"I was really looking forward to seeing you and hanging out." Evelyn pouted her disappointment at her friend.

"Well, since Hope has a mommy and daddy now, maybe she doesn't need Auntie Misty around so much." Misty waggled her brows at her. Evelyn's face grew hot at the suggestive faces her friend was pulling on the screen.

"Colt and I are just friends." The admission left a tight feeling in her chest, a yearning for something that was just out of reach.

"Oh." Misty's eyes grew wide as she suddenly remembered something. "I almost forgot to tell you. You remember Kelly? From the casino?"

"How could I forget her and Quinn? You did a fundraiser for her boyfriend, didn't you?"

"I did. Well, he asked her to marry him. All very romantic, I'm told. He got down on one knee and everything. A little birdie told me that Presley Barnett is going to be performing at the wedding. We are, of course, invited."

"Wow, that's great news." Evelyn was genuinely happy for Kelly. She'd seemed like a really nice lady. An unsettled feeling pushed down on her, making her feel edgy and out of sorts.

She stood and helped herself to the liquor cabinet. "Since you won't come here for the real thing, how about a virtual gals' drink?"

Misty's face brightened. "Let me go get a glass."

Knowing Colt had everything under control in the nursery, Evelyn poured herself a drink and made her way back to her chair. Maybe this would help with her inspiration and, in the very least, drive away the dreams of Colt that visited her each night in her sleep. She didn't want the fantasy Colt. She wanted the real thing. Raising the glass to her lips, she downed the contents. *Who am I kidding? Fantasy Colt is all I get.*

CHAPTER 16

Trixie was going to have everyone's hides when she got back from shopping. Colt stared glumly at the chaos. Her beloved, pristine kitchen looked like it had hosted a vegetarian frat party, and right at its epicenter sat one determined little miss.

Evelyn impatiently brushed a strand of hair away from her face with the back of her hand, her expression set as if going to battle. "I thought this was meant to be a straightforward process." She glared at him like he'd misled her.

Colt quickly scanned the book again. "It says baby fed weaning is ideal as it lets the baby feed itself finger food right from the start." He swore Hope raised her brow at him in a challenge. "Maybe she doesn't know that it's food we're offering?"

"Maybe she's stubborn like the rest of her family." Evelyn wearily sunk into a seat beside the highchair, his niece still not surrendering. "Whose idea was this anyway?"

"I believe it was yours. Something you read on a baby forum." Colt walked closer, holding the book in front of him like a shield. Hope giggled and waved at him. He wasn't going to be fooled by her cuteness. He'd made that mistake early on and had the stain on his shirt to prove it. "You know, we can just try a puree."

"But everything I read says finger food is the best thing for her."

He was alarmed to see tears beginning to shimmer in Evelyn's eyes. His stomach twisted into an anxious knot. Uncertainly, he peered at her. "Look at her little pudding belly. The kid isn't starving."

"Yes, but I just want the best for her." Evelyn sniffed. "I don't know what I'm doing. I don't have any of the mothering instincts that kick in when you have a baby."

"I'm fairly certain that's a myth." Giving a warning glare at Hope threatening dire action if anything was to be thrown his way, he scooted closer to Evelyn. "Look, Evelyn, Indie was Hope's mom, but so are you. She's lucky that you care so much that you read forums and books and everything. Lord knows I'm not. Well, except for that one I found in the attic by Doctor Spock. I guess what I'm saying is that Indie was upset she couldn't breastfeed her, but look at how well she did on formula. And now you want to do this baby led weaning thing, but how about we try puree and bits of food? We'll just do things our way, and as long as she's fed and loved, I think she'll live."

The tenderness in Evelyn's expression as she looked over at Hope amazed him. The fact that she looked at him the same way when she caught his eye made his heart skip a beat. "Thanks, Colt. I needed to hear that."

The slender delicate thread that was always there between them thickened, pulling him toward her. He cleared his throat. "Um, I was wondering if you'd given any thought to Christmas?"

Evelyn blinked, startled at the change in conversation. "I've got some gift ideas, but that's about it."

"I was thinking we should hold it here this year, invite everyone—and the Gray's, too. I think it would be good if they spent some time with their granddaughter."

She smiled as she nodded her agreement. "I think that's a great idea. I've been meaning to get in touch with the Gray's and arrange a visit. The last few times I called, they said they were busy, and I guess I just got busy too and forgot about it."

Colt started picking up bits of food from the floor, empathy for the elderly couple making guilt for his own behavior snake into a coil in the pit of his stomach. "I think I know why they're being like that. It's hard to let go of the pain. And you and I know that Bennett was everything to them. Sitting in that house, just the two of them, staring at the pictures up on the walls of him. I bet it must feel pretty grim. How about I go over and see them, ask them myself? Or better still, how about I invite them for a small family Thanksgiving—just us and them?"

"I think that's a marvelous idea. Something they won't feel overwhelmed by. I hope you can get through to them. They still have family who care about them, and I know Hope would make them feel better, maybe give them a reason to smile."

Evelyn reached out to him, and for a moment, he thought she was going to caress his cheek. Instead she plucked a piece of carrot from his collar. Added to his disappointment was a layer of guilt. He'd ruined any chance of something more between them the night he'd drunkenly kissed her. He'd wished he hadn't hurt her, but he didn't regret the kiss, not for one instant. In fact, it was the opposite. The rest of that horrible night might be a blur, but when he lay in bed at the end of each evening, he remembered that kiss crystal clear and it left him wanting more.

THE SHOCK of his truck hitting the rut almost ejected Colt from his seat. Everywhere, fences were in need of repair, weeds overtaking fields that had once had good grazing for stock. Not that he'd seen much stock on his drive to the Gray's homestead. Apparently, they'd sold most of them off. The closer he got to the house, the more despair and bleakness seeped into his bones. Bennet had helped his parents from time to time, especially when it was hay harvesting season, but Mr Gray had maintained the daily running of it and the old man's pride in his ranch had been legendary. In the little over a year since their son's death, it seemed like the heart had gone out of the countryside. The whole place seemed forlorn, broken. Colt sure as heck knew how that felt.

Shivering in apprehension of what was to greet him, Colt planted his hat firmly on his head like a knight girding himself in protective steel armor. Every sense tingled, warning that this was not going to go well. Stepping onto the porch, he could hear the sound of the television on inside the house. *A promising start.*

After several raps on the door went unanswered, he was just about to head around to the barn to see if perhaps Mr Gray was working in there, when the door opened. The disheveled old man's shirt was unbuttoned, showing a stained undershirt, beer can in hand. Bloodshot eyes glared at him.

"What do you want?"

Colt suddenly felt anxious to escape the other man's presence. "I came to see if you and Mrs Gray would like to come over to my ranch and spend Thanksgiving with us and Hope," he said as casually as he could manage.

"After all this time, you suddenly remember that we exist." There was no evading the accusations that burned from Mr Gray's eyes.

Colt felt uncomfortable. He spoke the truth. He hadn't seen or spoken to Bennett's parents since their grand-daughter was born. Heck, and only then via telephone. "You're right to be angry, but it wasn't deliberate. I just had some things I needed to work through."

"Wasn't deliberate? Some things to work through? Well, excuse me Mr Too-Busy-For-Us-Billionaire, but I find that I don't have time for you now."

"Mr Gray, I'm sorry. After Indie, well, I didn't handle things so good, and I know how you must be feeling with losing Bennett. If there's anything I can do ... how about I pay for a ranch hand for this place, help you get on top of things." Colt gestured to the sprawling mess that surrounded them, regretting it instantly when the old man's eyes snapped hatred at him.

"You can take your offer of help and your Thanksgiving invite and shove it right up your—" Mr Gray spluttered into a cough, his thin shoulders shaking with the violence of the spasm. "It ain't nothing but blood money."

"How is it blood money? It's an offer to help you." Colt reminded himself that the old man was grieving. Heck, it hadn't been that long ago that he'd felt much the same way about everything.

"We both know that if Bennett had never met you or your sister, he'd still be alive." Colt jerked back at the venomous words hurled at him.

"Jefferson, who is it?" Mrs Gray's tired voice called from inside.

"No one."

"Don't give me that. You're not that old and senile that you've started talking to yourself." Mrs Gray's silver-hair-topped face appeared at the screen door. "Hello, Colt, it's been a while."

"It has, ma'am." Colt quickly took his hat off his head, twisting its brim between his fingers.

"To what do we owe the pleasure?"

"He was just leaving," Mr Gray interrupted, jerking his chin toward Colt's truck like he needed assistance with the how.

"Yes, dear." Mrs Gray laid a hand on the screen. "But why did he visit?"

"I wanted to invite you and Mr Gray over for Thanksgiving. I know Hope would love to have her grandparents there." If looks could kill, the glare he was on the receiving end of from Mr Gray would have knocked him over stone cold.

"That's very nice of you. We'll have to talk it over."

Colt knew when he'd been dismissed. Placing his hat back on his head, he gave a nod to Mr Gray. "Hope to see you both there."

Long after he left, the look of bitterness and anger haunted Colt. Was that how he'd looked at Evelyn and Hope? It amazed him that Evelyn still spoke to him, and he was going to make sure every day that she didn't regret it. And he was beginning to think he had an idea how.

CHAPTER 17

$\mathcal{T}$he formal dining room was only ever used for, well, formal occasions. Evelyn much preferred—as did Colt—to have their meals at the table in the large kitchen. There was just something about the homely warmth that Trixie had created in her domain. But today the large snakewood table, its glossy reddish brown with contrasting black and chocolate patterned surface, was covered with gourds and an enormous cornucopia spilling sugar-art vegetables across the corn husks artfully dotted amongst the Thanksgiving décor.

Trixie had polished up the good china and crystal, the cutlery gleaming, ready to demolish the culinary delight that was to be served on it. Evelyn didn't even want to speculate just how expensive the tableware was. If she did, she'd be too scared to use any of it. Satisfied that everything was perfect for the umpteenth time, Evelyn checked the grandfather clock that stood to attention in the corner, disappointment turning her mouth down at the corners. It looked like the Gray's weren't going to come after all.

With a heavy sigh, she returned back to the formal lounge

where Colt lay stretched out on the rug before the crackling fireplace. She couldn't help but notice that his once freshly pressed shirt was now crumpled. She felt like crying as she took in the sight of Hope. The cute little mustard-colored dress she'd so carefully selected and the white tights that covered her chubby little legs somehow now had stains from the teething rusks she'd been gnawing at, and the headband with the little pumpkins on it that Evelyn had painstakingly set amongst her curls was completely missing in action. It was only the sight of Hope very seriously watching Colt stack blocks so she could knock them over that gave Evelyn any sense of joy for the day.

"You know, it was always a long shot having them come over." Colt gave her an understanding look. "You and Trixie put a lot of effort into making that spread we're going to have and I, for one, intend to enjoy every morsel that passes my lips." Hope clapped her hands together as the tower crashed to the floor. Colt stood up, gathering his niece on the way, and extended his hand to Evelyn. "Shall we go have ourselves a Thanksgiving feast?"

She smiled over her disappointment, careful not to show just how hurt she was by the Gray's rejection of Hope. "Well, I hope you enjoy it, because Trixie and I made enough to feed an army and it looks like we're all going to be eating it for days to come."

Colt wrapped an arm around her shoulders with Hope on his other hip like it was the most natural thing in the world. She drank in the comfort of his nearness as they made their way back down the hall from where she'd just come. It felt like she was floating. *Maybe it wasn't so bad that the Gray's had decided not to attend after all.* The thought of just the three of them having Thanksgiving as a little family—and, of course, Trixie, if they ever managed to extract her from the kitchen —was appealing.

The sound of the housekeeper rushing to answer the doorbell slowed the progress of the little trio. Disappointment swelled in her breast, followed by a chaser of guilt. The Gray's had obviously changed their minds and decided to attend, and it was something that would be good for everyone. She just needed to smother the flicker of regret at no longer having the intimate dinner she'd begun to envision.

Evelyn tried to ignore the strange aching in her heart as Colt's arm remained firmly in place when they turned to greet their guests. Mr and Mrs Gray both looked washed out, as if their grief had bleached the color from their appearance until all they had left only resembled their namesakes. Compassion welled up for the elderly couple, and she smiled in welcome at them.

"Hope, there are some people here who would love to meet you."

Mrs Gray's lower lip trembled as she stepped forward, not taking her gaze off the child. Hope held her arms out, and with a great rush, her grandmother gathered her close to her heart.

"Thank you for making us see past our sorrow and to see what we still had." Mrs Gray kissed the top of Hope's head. "I think I can see some of Bennett in her and, of course, lots of Indie." Despite her tear-filled, joyous eyes, the look she sent her husband nonetheless had an air of command. "Is there anything you'd like to say, dear?"

Mr Gray's face puckered like he'd sucked on a lemon. Finally, his gaze slid to meet Colt's. Evelyn couldn't be sure if what was to come out of his mouth was going to be pleasant. "We almost didn't come." His voice was rough and sharp, like old sandpaper. "In fact, if I'd had my way, we wouldn't have. But Mrs Gray, she said that if we didn't, we'd regret it. And seeing her with the baby, well, I reckon she was right. Bennett always thought of you as family and so do we. I reckon, like any family, we're allowed a quarrel or two." He stretched his hand out to Colt.

The silence hung awkwardly between them. Even Hope seemed to know that something important was happening and was quiet in Mrs Gray's arms. Colt swallowed, his hand tightening on her shoulder before releasing it to swing down to clasp the other man's hand tightly.

"I reckon you're right. We're still family, and we're glad you decided to join us for Thanksgiving. It looks like we might actually have a thing or two to be thankful for after all. Now, I think it's time we start eating. Trixie?" The house-keeper's head popped out of the kitchen. "Take off your apron. It's time to celebrate."

Evelyn gave Mrs Gray a smile, enjoying the color that had come to the other woman's cheeks. "Looks like Hope has made herself right at home. If you wouldn't mind taking her in, I'll help Trixie with the food."

A shimmer brightened the older lady's eyes. "It's been a while since I've held a little one—and she's almost not a baby anymore—but I think it'll come back to me. Evelyn?"

"Yes, Mrs Gray?"

"Thank you for loving my granddaughter when we couldn't."

Evelyn drew the frail woman close. "We're family, and that's what we do." She released her. "Now, go enjoy her while I get the food." Colt was right. They had plenty to be thankful for after all.

THERE IT WAS AGAIN—THAT need to touch Evelyn, his arm finding a way to gently encircle her waist as they stood on the porch waving goodbye to the Gray's.

"I think that went well." The way she snuggled into him as she waved was almost better than winning a gold buckle.

"Well, there was no blood. And honestly, after the reception I got when I went and asked the old coot, that surprised me." Hope nuzzled her face sleepily into Evelyn's shoulder. The poor kid was exhausted from all the attention she'd got. "How about you get her ready for bed and settled, and then you and I can have a night cap."

Her gaze flickered up to his before her dark lashes shielded them again, pink blooming on her cheeks. "I'd like that."

Colt watched her leave. Yep, Evelyn Hart sure was something, and it was about time he did something about it.

Heading into the library, he perused the selection of liquor. His original idea of champagne seemed too flashy, like there was something big to be celebrated. No, this needed to be more subtle. Colt's hand came to rest on a red calf leather covered box. Opening it, he considered the crystal and silver decanter that lay nestled in a bed of silver silk and velvet. *Yes, the Legacy Rum by Angostura would do nicely.* Freeing it from its luxurious confinement, he snagged two crystal decanters and settled himself in front of the fire. He briefly wondered if he should dim the lights, but quickly discarded it as too obvious a mood setter. Strangely, it was important to Colt that whatever happened tonight—whatever was said—was authentic.

"COLT!" His heart leapt from his chest, his feet hitting the floor before he had time to think. "Colt! Where are you? Something's wrong with Hope." Blindly, he followed the sound of her scared voice. "Oh no. Something's really wrong. Hope, darling, can you hear me? I'm right here, baby girl."

He found her clutching a limp Hope wrapped in a towel to her chest. "Evelyn, what happened?" Fear made his voice rough over his pounding heart.

"I was giving her a quick bath because I thought she was all sticky from dinner. She had a little rash, but I thought that was from her diaper. I started washing her, and the rash got worse, spreading all over her body, and she got really hot. So I thought I would start drying her and get some medicine to help with the temperature, and then she had something like a spasm." Evelyn began to cry. "I don't know what's wrong with her."

Colt took Hope from her and opened the towel to reveal the mottled pattern covering her torso and extending out to her limbs. Her chest rose and fell in shallow breaths. *At least she's breathing.* "Evelyn, we need to get to her to hospital right away. Quickly grab what you need, and I'll take her to my truck and get it started."

"Is she going to be okay?" The way Evelyn looked at him —as if she had all her faith in him—was terrifying.

"I don't know. But we need to get her to hospital straight-away." Without another word, he turned and madly bolted, his precious cargo clutched tightly to his chest. *Indie and Bennett, if you're up there, I need your help right about now. Don't let me down.*

Colt didn't think he would ever recover from the trauma of seeing Hope being held by Evelyn as IV lines were inserted into her tiny arm, nor the sight of the oxygen mask covering her pale face as she lay deathly still, looking fragile and small on the hospital bed. Evelyn wrapped an arm protectively around her, and Hope snuggled into her familiar warmth before drifting off to sleep again.

"Mr Montgomery, Ms Hart," the doctor finally addressed them. "She's a sick little girl right now, but she's getting fluids, and I've given her something that will help lower her temperature. The good news is that it looks worse than it is and by tomorrow she'll be much improved."

"What's wrong with her?" Evelyn's voice trembled. Colt

was envious that she could show her fear. He knew he needed to be the strong one. Later, he would have time to fall apart, but not right now.

"Hope has Adenovirus. From the name you can probably gather it's a viral infection. The spasms and rash were both from the extremely high temperature she had."

"But she's going to be all right now." Colt desperately needed to hear the doctor say it again. The fear of something happening to his little Hope … well, he'd go past the brink of darkness and not return if something did.

"Yes, she'll be fine. In fact, in a day or two, you won't even know she was sick."

"Thank God," cried Evelyn, smothering Hope's forehead in kisses. "You scared the living daylights out of me, Hope. I swear I'm too young for the gray hairs you gave me tonight."

The doctor, knowing he was no longer needed, exited the room, leaving Colt alone with his family. The thought of something happening to any of his girls shattered him, tearing at his insides. He loved them too much to allow it. He sat beside Evelyn, wrapping an arm around her and stretching his free hand out to lay it over hers. Right now, he needed to touch her, gather them both close.

"I promise I won't ever let anything happen. Not to you, and not to our Hope."

Her beautiful blue eyes simmered like deep pools after a thunderstorm. It was too easy to lose himself in the way she looked at him. But maybe he was lost already, and he didn't mind one bit.

CHAPTER 18

*C*risp frostiness hung heavy in the air, heralding in the start of the holiday season. As stockings were hung and decorations unpacked, Colt found his gaze always drifting back to Evelyn. He'd always known there was something special about her. Heck, a blind man could see that. And yet, now she seemed to fill every part of him. She was his greatest addiction, and he was at a loss at how to move from the comfortable friendship they'd settled into with their little family into something passionate and intimate. The thought of waking up to Evelyn in his bed, holding her—

"Colt, if you let go of that angel where you've got it, it's gonna break."

Colt blinked back to reality, finding a perplexed Evelyn staring up at him from the bottom of the ladder he was standing on. He looked to where he was holding the Christmas angel a good ten inches from the tree, prepared to let it go. He shook his head. Dang, he needed to get a grip.

"Logan finally got back to me and said he and Shelby will be over for lunch. They're going to their parents first in the morning and then they'll be straight over."

She frowned up at him as he carefully lowered the ornament into position. "I hope he told them they were more than welcome to come for lunch as well."

"He always does, but I think his parents like to visit his grandparents at the nursing home for lunch. Does the angel look like it's leaning? I hope I didn't get the drunk one by mistake."

Evelyn stepped away from the tree, careful not to tread on Hope where she was playing, rolling ornaments back and forth. With a practiced eye she gauged the angle. "Your angel's perfect."

Colt grinned back at her and gave her his best smirk. "She always has been."

Color flooded her cheeks. She was adorable as she nibbled her bottom lip. "I was talking about the angel," she spluttered, pointing at the top of the tree.

"So was I." He jumped down from the ladder, and she gave a little shriek of surprise when he picked her up in his arms and turned her to face Hope. "Isn't Mommy Evelyn pretty?"

The little girl stared up at them with the solemn eyes that only an almost-one-year-old could give. "Pret Pret."

"That's right, Hope, she's very pret pret."

"Put me down, you big lug. And no fair bringing Hope into it."

Colt reluctantly settled Evelyn back on her own two feet. "Hope agreed because it's the truth."

Evelyn smoothed her hair down, a flustered expression on her face. "Well, I don't know about that. Now, finish putting these decorations up. At this rate, we won't get them done before everyone arrives, and that's still a couple of weeks away."

"Aye aye, ma'am." Colt gave her a salute and then winked at Hope, setting the child to giggling. *Yep, life was good. Very good indeed.*

Once the holiday season was in full swing, it flew by in a flurry of fairy lights and tinsel as it tends to do. Before Colt knew it, it was the day before Christmas, and he'd still not managed to find the perfect time to tell Evelyn how he felt. Now that everyone had arrived, it seemed even less likely that it would happen anytime soon. He loped Big Wheels around, the horse snorting steam like a fairytale dragon as Logan swung a rope. They'd never had a holiday gathering without undertaking a quick roping challenge. From memory, Colt was the reigning twenty times Christmas Buckle Champion.

On the sidelines, the girls were well rugged up against the chill in the air. Hope looked like a teddy bear with a little knit cap with twin pompoms on top. Evelyn gave him a smile that filled him with a toasty warmth like only the best brandy could. Beside her, Misty rubbed her hands together and cast daggers at Logan. Shelby, Logan's sister was sitting on the rail in what looked to be a jacket she'd inherited from her brother and an old trucker cap. Both her and Logan would head home after dinner to spend the rest of Christmas Eve and Morning with their parents.

"You're almost as slow as Bennett was," Colt teased, enjoying the way the rope snarled. Logan muttered a string of curses that would have been enough to make a sailor blush. "At least he actually managed to be competition once he got himself organized. Or are all the dirty looks Misty's throwing your way putting you off your game?"

"Shut up." Logan's eyes guiltily jerked to Misty.

Interesting. "There's a story there that you haven't gotten around to telling me."

"I don't know what you're talking about." Logan clamped his mouth mulishly together, resolutely looking in the opposite direction to Misty.

"Oh, you wanna play it like that?" Colt couldn't resist tweaking his friend's nose. It was Christmas, after all. "How about I go over there and ask Misty myself?"

Logan's eyes narrowed. "Don't you dare!"

Colt smiled merrily at him and clucked Big Wheels forward. "Watch me." The big chestnut loped over to the girls, Hope waving her arms at him. He bent forward and took her from Evelyn, gently placing her in front of him in the saddle. "How's my little cowgirl?" He solemnly tipped his hat to the women. "Ladies. Hope, I swear your Mommy Evelyn is the prettiest cowgirl I've ever seen."

"And he should know. He's been up close to quite a few of them," Logan muttered, having finally regained his composure enough to join them.

Colt smirked at him. "That makes me an expert then." Evelyn's cheeks—already pinkened from the chilled air—deepened in color and she laughed at him, waving the compliment off, her eyes bright with merriment. She wasn't merely pretty. She was gorgeously magnetic, compelling his gaze to always return to her.

"If you're done stalling, I thought we were here to do some roping," Logan groused, sore at being closer to the venom Misty's eyes were spitting at him.

"You were the one taking his sweet time with the rope. I thought I'd find some more pleasant company while I waited." Colt winked at Evelyn, his eyes drinking her up. "But if you're finally ready, I guess we'd best get started." He gave Hope a quick hug before handing her carefully back to Evelyn. A question he saw in her eyes startled him. Maybe it was time to have that talk after all.

～

"WHEN DID you and Colt get together?" Shelby asked as she handed the peas over to Mrs Gray. Evelyn choked on her mouthful of food, Misty helpfully thumping her on the back as Colt grinned like a Cheshire cat.

"Um, we're not," Evelyn finally managed, wiping the tears from her face as she reached for her wineglass.

"Oh, I just assumed, you know, with all the long, dramatic looks between the two of you when you think no one is looking." Shelby shrugged and reached for the carrots.

"Or all the touching," Misty agreed. "I mean, I haven't been here that much the last couple of months, but when did that start happening?"

"Mr Gray and I just assumed the two of you were together now, given how you're raising Hope as a family," Mrs Gray agreed.

"Yeah, Colt, is there anything you want to tell us?" Logan nudged his friend in the side. Evelyn wanted the floor to open up and swallow her, not knowing where to look.

"Evelyn and I are close. We always have been, and now we have a little girl who is our priority. That's all there is to tell." Evelyn tried to hide how much Colt's casual dismissal of them being together hurt. It's not like he wasn't telling the truth. But still, her heart froze.

"I mean, it was bad enough having to sit through Bennett and Indie and all the puppy dog eyes they used to throw at each other." Shelby pulled a disgusted face. "I don't know if I have the stomach to go through that again."

"Remember the Christmas they first got together and they wore matching sweaters for the whole holidays?" Misty said. "They must have spent a fortune on them."

"They did," Colt replied dryly. "She put them on my credit card."

"They looked so sweet together." Mrs Gray smiled at the

memory. "Until Bennett somehow got his braces tangled in her sweater."

"I'd forgotten that." Logan roared with laughter. "We had to cut him free, and Indie wouldn't look at us for the rest of the holidays. I've lost count of how many times we had to keep saving them from their braces."

"You can't talk," Colt said, raising his eyebrows in challenge. "I remember when one Christmas Eve you and Misty went missing and we found you stuck in the hayloft because the old ladder had somehow got knocked over."

"Yeah, well, we don't need to talk about that," Misty muttered.

"Are you sure? Cause I'd like to talk about it sometime." Logan's mouth worked as he glared at Misty across the table.

Mr Gray cleared his throat. "Thank you for Christmas Eve dinner, but Mrs Gray and I should be heading home. What time would you like us back here tomorrow?"

"Anytime. If you come early, we can wait to open gifts till you arrive," offered Evelyn. "I know Santa is going to bring lots of presents for Hope's first Christmas." She gave Colt a long-suffering look. "Now for Santa to help wrap them all." Colt gave her a wink over his wineglass and her heart fluttered at the warmth in his eyes.

"We should be going too," Logan said, rising. "Mom said that her and Dad were planning on a late cup of eggnog. It might be nice to join them."

"She didn't tell me that," Shelby huffed. "And I'm the one who likes it more than you do."

"No, you don't." Logan glared at his sister.

"Whatever." Shelby poked her tongue out at him.

"Children, play nice and say goodnight." Mrs Gray began to usher them from the room to a chorus of farewells and promises to return bright and early.

"I still say there's something going on," Shelby said to her brother as they disappeared from sight. Evelyn's eyes skittered to Colt only to discover him watching her with an intense look that thrilled her to her toes.

Misty sighed. "I never thought they'd leave." She glanced up, catching the look between them. "And that's my cue to say I still have some things to do and say my goodnight."

"You don't have to go." The words sounded insincere even to Evelyn's ears.

"Yes, I do. And taking a page out of Mrs Gray's book, play nice, kids." Misty gave them both a naughty grin before flouncing from the room.

"Subtlety was never one of Misty's strong points." Colt chuckled. "But I do like how she thinks."

Evelyn felt her stomach flutter, a tingle going through her. "We still need to wrap those presents tonight."

"If I'm a good boy, can I unwrap mine early?" She couldn't deny the spark of excitement at the double meaning of his words.

"Colt Montgomery, I'm not sure if you're on Santa's naughty or nice list."

"Maybe I'm on both." He came closer until she could feel the warmth of his body. "You know Shelby was right. There's something between us."

"I mean, we have Hope." She stalled, not sure if she was brave enough to agree.

His hand gently caressed the back of her neck. "Yes, we have Hope. But what I'm talking about is between you and me."

Evelyn licked her lips, her heart screaming at her to tell him. "I'm worried that what's going on—how I feel—it might be that we're clinging together, trying to weather the storm of grief."

Her cheeks grew hot under the heat of his gaze. "It's real, and it's something I want to explore with you."

She felt her blood coursing through her veins like an awakened river as Colt lowered his head. He pressed his lips to hers, more caressing her mouth than kissing it. Evelyn's senses reeled as if short-circuited. Raising his mouth from hers, he gazed into her eyes.

"I have no doubts. Do you?"

She stared at him, a burning desire filling her, a need for him to kiss her again. "No."

The way he smiled at her, like he'd just won the championship of a lifetime, made her insides quiver. Colt's lips recaptured hers, more demanding this time, and she was powerless to resist, her entire soul consumed by him. She was his, and she always had been.

CHAPTER 19

"Colt," breathed Evelyn. "Where did all the extra gifts come from?" She stared around the room, agog at all the glistening bows and wrapped boxes covering every available surface. "I thought we put everything out last night."

His green eyes sparkled like a little boy who had just pulled off the ultimate surprise—which he had—all the while striving to be the very image of innocence. "I don't know anything about this. You'll have to ask Santa." He set Hope down on the plush cashmere silk carpet and she bottom-scooted her way to the nearest present, gravely inspecting the bow, her little face a picture of concentration.

"I think she's going to need help opening everything." Evelyn knew Colt had money—heck, the house they lived in was huge—but it was easy to forget. Until he did something like this, and she was reminded once again that he was a billionaire.

"Who says they're all for her? Maybe a certain beautiful lady made it on the nice list this year, too." The way he looked at her warmed her to her very toes. "Before everyone arrives, there's something I'd like to give you first."

"Oh, well, then I'd like to give you my gift as well." Evelyn quickly retrieved a box wrapped in silvery blue wrapping paper, a large pearl white ribbon adorning it. "Would you like to go first?"

"No, you can go first," Colt answered quickly, the words spilling from his lips.

Evelyn tilted her head as she took in his flushed features. Handing her gift to him, she prayed he liked it. Colt sat down beside Hope and carefully unwrapped the ribbon before lifting the lid of the box free to reveal silver tissue paper. He hesitated, looking up, a question in his gaze. She smiled back at him, nervous now that the moment was here. Slowly, he peeled away the gossamer covering to reveal a glass sculpture.

"It's beautiful," he said, peering into its translucent depths. "I hear the artist is quite respected in the art world."

Evelyn dropped cross-legged to the floor beside him, Hope pulling herself into her lap. "You see the red heart right in the center of the child in the middle?"

"Yes."

"That's Hope's soul. And then the swirl of yellow and green around that? That's Indie and Bennett holding her close, always in her heart." She swallowed, worried now that the piece was too intimate. She felt vulnerable. "The two people holding her represent you and me, and the fact that we're a family." Embarrassed, she looked away.

A gentle hand on her chin guided her gaze back to his. "I love it." Careful not to squish the child on her lap, he leaned forward and gave her a soft kiss. "And now it's my turn."

"I hope we didn't come over too early, but we didn't want Hope to have to wait to open her presents," Mrs Gray said as her and Mr Gray bustled into the room, arms laden with more gifts.

Evelyn couldn't be sure, but she thought she heard Colt sigh in frustration before he smoothly rose to his feet and greeted his guests. "Not at all. In fact, I think Hope is going to need some help from her grandparents."

Colt sent her a helpless shrug. Obviously, what he wanted to give her would have to wait, but why? Before long, the room was filled with laughter and chatter as Misty came downstairs, still clad in her pajamas, more gifts in her arms. Bryce and Savannah had sent the cutest little cowgirl outfit, complete with boots and hat and the promise to catch up in the New Year. Hope was still opening her presents when Logan and Shelby arrived with yet more gifts. One thing was for certain—Hope had enough to last her for a long time to come.

"Do you want me to go get it ready?" Logan asked Colt, glancing out the window.

"I think it's almost time." Colt caught her gaze and quickly looked away guiltily. *What were those two up to?* She curiously watched as Logan slipped from the room before returning to watching Hope playing in the discarded wrapping paper, oblivious to the presents stacked beside her.

Colt cleared his throat. "If everyone wants to come with me, I think Hope might have one more present." He scooped Hope up into his arms, and with the guests following him, he led them outside, looking around expectantly. When nothing appeared, he frowned, looking at the barn. "I guess we should go over there." Evelyn swore she heard him muttering about never relying on Logan if you want it done right. Just as they were a few feet away, Logan appeared from the shadows of the large building, a little white spotted pony trailing behind him decked out in a pink western saddle.

Evelyn blinked at the sight. "You got Hope her own pony?"

"Well, she can't be a cowgirl if she doesn't have her own pony, right?" Colt puffed his chest out, appearing quite satisfied with himself.

"She can't even walk yet."

"It won't be long. Anyway, she's very good at sitting, and that's all she needs to do to begin with. Sit in the saddle and hold on." Colt grinned down at the little girl. "Shall we go say hello to Freckles?"

"Freckles?" Misty snorted. "The pony is called Freckles."

"It is very cute," Mrs Gray said, "and the little pink saddle is darling. Hope, come to Grandma and we'll go say hello to Freckles."

Evelyn shook her head in mock defeat. "Looks like I've been outvoted."

Colt put an arm around her, pulling her in close. "This time. But you were never going to win against a cute pony with a pink saddle."

She sighed again. "I guess not. Good thing you're cute, too."

He kissed the top of her head. "I try."

COLT BREATHED in the smell of Evelyn's hair as they stood together watching the scene unfold before them, her curves fitting snugly into him like she'd been molded with him in mind. He liked the thought of that.

"Evelyn," Misty called, waving her over. "Come here and get in the photo."

Apologetically, she looked up at him. He understood. He didn't want to stop touching her either. "Better not keep Misty waiting. She's scary when she's mad, just ask Logan."

Evelyn's eyes sparkled with mirth. "Has he ever said why? Misty clams up whenever I ask."

"It must be juicy if neither of them will say. Now scoot and get in that picture." He patted her on the behind, making her shriek with laughter as she hurried forward.

Mr Gray, seeing an opportunity, made his way away from the crowd around Hope and her pony. Awkwardly, the two of them stood in silence. Colt decided to throw the old man a bone.

"I'm glad you've decided to be part of Hope's life."

"Yeah, the missus can't stop talking about her. I don't think I've seen her this happy since—" Mr Gray cleared his throat. "Well, for some time."

"Yeah, Hope tends to have that effect on people. Give her enough time, and she wears everyone down into loving her." It seemed like a distant memory now, all the anger and hatred he'd felt toward her. He was ashamed at how he'd behaved, but there was nothing he could do about the past. He sure as heck was going to make sure the future was very different.

"I wanted to apologize for my behavior when you came out to the ranch." Mr Gray's eyes never strayed from in front of him. "Some of the things I said, they were uncalled for."

"You have no need to apologize," Colt said. Hope kept grabbing a handful of Freckles's ear and pulling it before Logan could extract the pony from her grasp. "I understand. I've been there myself."

Mr Gray's expression was one of mute wretchedness. "How do you get over it?"

Colt looked at where Hope was now held in Evelyn's arms, Misty making faces to get the little girl to giggle. "Love. I reckon that's the only thing powerful enough to heal hurt that bad."

The old man nodded, digesting his words. "Mrs Gray

reckons I'm a stubborn old fool and that my pride will be the death of me. Maybe she's right. But if the offer's still there, I reckon I could use a hand on the ranch."

"I'll have a ranch hand there next week," Colt promised. "Now, if you'll excuse me, there's something I need to take care of."

"Sure thing, Colt, and thanks again."

The way Evelyn smiled at him when he walked over set his heart to hammering in his chest, bottling all the words up in his throat. Quizzically, she stared at him, waiting for him to speak.

"Dude, are you just going to stand there?" Logan gave him a nudge.

Colt had never been so grateful to his friend, the teasing allowing him to find his voice again. "Can I steal Evelyn and Hope away for a moment? I promise I'll bring them right back. And in the meantime, Logan can put Freckles away and everyone else can help themselves to some eggnog or mulled wine in the dining room."

"Oh, can he now?" Logan muttered good-naturedly as he led the pony away.

Colt took Hope from Evelyn and placed her on his hip, his free hand reaching down to clasp Evelyn's cold one. Without a word, he led them back into the house to stand in front of the roaring fire. "Let me take your jacket." He helped her divest herself of the garment before doing the same for Hope.

The gift wrapping crinkled underfoot as he made himself back to them. The light of the fire made Evelyn's dark hair ripple and shimmer, the warmth giving a pink glow to her heart-shaped face. Large periwinkle blue eyes watched him, an expectant sparkle making his heart beat faster.

Fear spiked through him. What if he got this wrong? "I should have written something down," he muttered.

She raised a brow at him, her mouth quirking. "Write what down?"

"It doesn't matter." He wished he'd had the forethought to grab a drink. His throat now felt dry, his tongue thick in his mouth. He swallowed again. If he didn't say this soon, he was going to chicken out. "Evelyn, everyone I love has been taken away from me, and how I feel about you, that scares me. But being with you soothes my soul. I love you."

Tenderly, Evelyn stroked his cheek. "Oh, Colt. I love you too, for all of my life it feels like."

He looked down at the envelope he held in his hands. "This is for you. Merry Christmas."

Her beautiful face scrunched up as she opened it, she glanced up at him and then down again. "What is this?"

"It's adoption paperwork for Hope. It has both of our names on it."

Her mouth dropped open, her eyes turning into blue pools as tears shimmered. "Colt." His name was a breathy whisper. "Do you really mean this?"

His own tears stung his eyes. "I really do. I guess all that's left is how you're going to sign it."

"What do you mean?"

"With your old name or your new one. I think Evelyn Montgomery has a nice ring to it." He grinned down at Hope. "Speaking of rings... Okay, Hope, just like we've been practicing." He placed a little box in the girl's hand and, grasping her other one, helped her waddle toward Evelyn, holding it out in front of her proudly.

Evelyn's bottom lip trembled as, with a cry, she gathered the little girl up in her arms. Colt took it from her and went down on one knee, opening the box to reveal a black diamond larger than a quail's egg surrounded by brilliant sapphires. "You took the pieces of my heart and put them back together. Even if you had to smack some sense into me along the way. Without your love, I would have lost the last bit of my family and you. Will you marry me, Evelyn, the keeper now and forever of my heart?"

Tears streamed down her face. "Yes." She fanned herself. "You've made me a complete mess, but yes. I love you, Colt." He slipped the ring on her finger. "Colt, I can barely lift my hand under all the rocks you've just put on it."

A smile tugged at his lips. "You remember when I said I had all this money and didn't know what to spend it on? I think I've just found my new addiction. How about we fly to Paris and buy matching outfits for you and Hope? In fact, why don't we buy our own plane? It would make it easier for all the shopping trips I plan on taking my girls on." Evelyn laughed his silliness away—at least, she must have thought he'd been joking...

Colt pulled her close, Hope touching Evelyn's tears with her finger. "I think I should give Mommy Evelyn a kiss now, don't you, Hope?"

Tenderly, he raised Evelyn's chin with his hand and claimed her lips. Somewhere, he knew his parents were watching, arm in arm, alongside Bennett and Indie. And as he lost himself to the kiss, he could feel their loving approval. It was like he'd told Mr Gray. All the pain he'd carried all his life, so much that he'd just gotten used to it until it had broken him, it was love that had mended it. Only love that was strong enough. The love of Evelyn.

THE END

AS AN INDIE AUTHOR, reviews help me get my books noticed. If you enjoyed reading Colt and Evelyn's story as much as I did writing it, please leave a review. It will make all the difference to me.

If you loved, *The Wounded Cowboy Billionaire,* sign up for my newsletter here to get the free bonus Art Exhibition Scene. Now, turn the page to discover Misty and Logan's Story, *The Billionairess' Cowboy*

SNEAK PEEK – THE BILLIONAIRESS' COWBOY

"*I*f you can make sure we have the latest patches for that software before Tuesday, that would be great." Misty swiveled her chair slightly, moving her gaze to the suavely dressed man beside her. "William, is there anything else you want to add?" She left the question hanging.

Her business partner pursed his soft lips in thought. *I swear the man uses more lip balm than I do.* "No, I think you've covered it all for the moment."

Dana, Misty's PA, discreetly entered the room, dipping her perfectly coiffured head down to her boss's ear. "Your driver is ready to take you to the airport."

Misty nodded her wordless thanks. "Folks, if no one has anything else they want to add, I'm happy to end this meeting."

"You would." William looked up from the manicured nail he'd been inspecting. "Off to play in the dirt again."

"I'd hardly say going to a billionaire's ranch is playing in the dirt," she retorted, gathering her devices from the table.

"Anyway, I mainly stay in the house with Evelyn and the baby."

"Well, don't come back bringing any of that farmyard smell with you." William wrinkled his nose up in mock protest.

"You wouldn't be able to smell it over your own cologne," Misty tartly replied. She loved her business partner, but he could be such a prima donna sometimes and yet the ladies seemed to eat it up. Each to their own, she guessed, but she liked her men to be real men with calloused hands and five o'clock stubble. *Like Logan*, an irritating voice in her mind whispered.

Shoving her chair into place a little harder than warranted, she spun on her Louboutin's and marched across the polished ebony floor to the door. Misty rather enjoyed the way the silk lining of her skirt slid against her skin as each stride sent a loud *click clack* through the respectfully quiet room. Wealth had its privileges, so did power. And she had both in spades.

"Dana," Misty said, not surprised to have her PA materialize at her side. "Can you please make sure that I'm not disturbed this weekend? Anything that is urgent can be forwarded to William." She laughed at the droll expression on the other woman's face. Dana had discovered the rare combination of plastic surgery and still remaining fairly natural in a much better-looking version of herself.

"I expect an enormous bonus this year for all the complaining I'll have to put up with," Dana deadpanned. "Now, the plane is stocked with your favorite beverages and I've also arranged a salad from the restaurant you like waiting for your pleasure once you're in the air. Is there anything else you need me to organize?"

"No, I think that's everything."

"Excellent. Then have a safe flight, and I'll see you on

Monday morning." Dana pushed the elevator button for her boss and stepped to one side.

"Thank you, I'll see you in a few days' time."

The elevator doors opened, and Misty stepped inside, praying they would close before someone could find her and delay her with last minute issues. It was with a sense of relief that she felt the familiar plummeting sensation of descent. A few quick minutes after that, she was settled in her town car and being driven away. Misty watched as the cityscape rose up around her, the skyscrapers clawing at the heavens, filled with thousands of people toiling away at their tasks. *Well, not all of them,* she corrected herself. *Some were filled with millionaires and fewer still with billionaires, slaves to their wealth and status.*

She knew how that felt. It was why it was so important to her to make sure she headed back to Colt's family ranch. Her best friend, Evelyn, was waiting for her there, ready to celebrate Hope's first birthday. Misty hadn't been there since Christmas, and she wasn't going to miss this event for the world. Even if it meant having to see Logan Erikson.

The Billionairess' Cowboy available on Amazon and in Kindle Unlimited here

ACKNOWLEDGMENTS

A debt of gratitude to my editor Rebekah Groves for her patience with me.

Another big thanks to Megan from Designed with Grace for her cover design.

To my amazing beta readers and street team, you guys rock and I couldn't do it without you. Special mention to Lisa and Cair.

And finally to my fabulous alpha reader Trixie Norman, for all the late nights of reading and endless questions about your thoughts.

ALSO BY EDITH MACKENZIE

Have you read them all?

Billionaire Hearts Ranch Series

A Cowboy's Riches (Prequel)

She's broken free and is ready to fly…or ride, as the case may be…

Buy Now

The Wounded Cowboy Billionaire

He had all the money in the world—and it wasn't enough to keep his life from falling apart…

Buy Now

The Billionairess' Cowboy

He broke her heart once. She's not about to let him do it again…

Buy Now

The Billionaire's Cowgirl

Shelby and William's story coming soon

Buy Now

The Cowgirl's Fake Billionaire Marriage

Chora's story coming soon

Buy Now

Barrels and Hearts Series

A Bull Rider's Paradise

The prequel to the Barrels and Hearts series. True love is only the beginning….of the story. Find out where it all began with Ana and Eduardo. Sometimes finding love is easy. It's keeping it that's hard.

Buy here

A Cowgirl's Dream

An Aussie cowgirl far from home. A handsome Brazilian bull rider. Can they have a rodeo love story of their dreams?

Buy Now

A Cowgirl's Heart

An Aussie cowgirl in need. Her childhood friend to the rescue. Can friendship turn into a love story?

Buy Now

A Cowgirl's Passion

One feisty cowgirl. One steadfast Brazilian bull rider. Will she see what is right in front of her?

Buy Now

A Cowgirl's Pride

An Aussie cowgirl from the wrong side of the tracks. A handsome equine vet. Can they find a way to have their happy ever after?

Buy Now

A Cowgirl's Love

A young Aussie cowgirl. A widowed rancher. Does age matter when it comes to love?

Buy Now

A Cowgirl's Movie Star

A fiery cowgirl with big dreams. A movie star far from home. When their two worlds collide, will their love be strong enough to hold them together or will they be pulled apart

Buy Now

A Cowgirl's Billionaire

A cowgirl adrift. A broken billionaire cowboy. Can he free himself from the past to be the man she needs now?

Buy Now

Cowboy Christmas Series

The Mistletoe Collection

Boots and Mistletoe

Cowboy boots, mistletoe, and a holiday do-over…

Buy Now

The Cowboy Under the Mistletoe

It'll take more than the magic of the season to help this grump find her happily ever after…

Buy Now

Mistletoe and the Billionaire's Cowgirl

He's the last man she wants this holiday season. Too bad he's exactly what she needs…

Buy Now

ABOUT THE AUTHOR

Edith MacKenzie or Eddie Mac to her friends is an author of sweet and wholesome contemporary cowboy romance. They say in literary circles to write what you know, and Eddie has certainly taken that to heart. Before embarking on a writing career, she trained horses professionally and brings that wealth of knowledge to her writing.

Now a mum to a boy and girl, as well as wife, she delights with her tales of strong cowgirls and their adventures in finding love. When not weaving the love stories of her characters, she enjoys hanging out with her family and animals, as well as reading, fishing and camping.

Just remember—once a cowgirl, always a cowgirl.

facebook.com/EddieMacAuthor

instagram.com/edith_mackenzie_author

amazon.com/Edith-MacKenzie

bookbub.com/profile/edith-mackenzie

twitter.com/edith_mackenzie

Made in the USA
Las Vegas, NV
07 January 2022

40707406R00100